ADAPTATION

BOOK TWO OF THE EMPTY BODIES SERIES

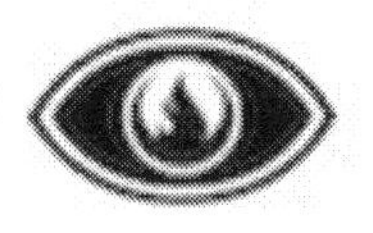

Zach Bohannon

EMPTY BODIES 2: ADAPTATION

Zach Bohannon

www.zachbohannon.com

Edited and Proofread by:

Jennifer Collins

Christy McQuire

Cover design by Johnny Digges

www.diggescreative.com

"Zach comes out with suspense that will haunt you, and you won't be able to look away."
J. Thorn, Amazon Top 100 Horror Author

"Few horror writers work as hard as Zach Bohannon. Turn the lights low, and don't let the blood splatter hit you."
Dan Padavona, author of *Storberry*

"Bohannon's *Empty Bodies* is dark, enthralling, and offers an impressive look into a terrifying post-apocalyptic world."
Taylor Krauss, Horror Blogger

"Zach Bohannon takes dark thriller and suspense to a terrifying new level, with spine tingling tales of the macabre that will keep you turning the page deep into the night."
David J. Delaney, Author of *The Vanishing*

For the readers:
Thank you.

PROLOGUE

The place they brought him to was cold and no light peeked in under the blindfold, so he assumed that it was also dark. They hadn't taken the blindfold off of him since they brought him here, so he couldn't know for sure, not that it mattered.

It had been hours since the men had visited. Hours since they had brought food or water. His lips were dry and his stomach growled, which he could hear every now and again.

He wasn't the only one they'd brought here.

He'd counted at least three others. Two of them he guessed to be girls from the higher pitched mumble through their gags, and the other was definitely a man. For whatever reason, they hadn't gagged the man like they had him and the two girls, but the man didn't ever yell or cry out. He remained calm, now and then mumbling scripture to himself and praying.

The door opened.

A gentle breeze hit his face and he heard at least two dogs barking. The girls tried to scream through their gags but they were muted. He was doing the same as his heart raced and he pissed himself, again.

The barking was getting closer. Before he knew it, he felt a wet nose on his leg and one of the dogs was sniffing the piss that had run down to his shin.

"Come on, you little shit," a male voice demanded. The dog pulled away from his leg and began to bark again, and the prisoner jolted. His hands were tied above his head and his feet barely touched the ground, leaving him vulnerable to whatever these people or dogs wanted to do to him.

He stopped trying to vocalize through the sock stuffed in his mouth when he heard another type of growl.

It was familiar.

It was one of *them*.

The thing snarled and the sound was unmistakable. It lurked closer until it stopped just a few feet in front of where the prisoners were restrained. All four of them were silent now, other than the trembling that came through their heavy breathing.

"You got 'em?" a man asked.

"Yeah, yeah. Get those ready."

Chains rustled and he heard one of the girls yelp through her gag. The snarling intensified and it sounded as if the men were struggling.

"Hold him!"

"I'm fucking trying! Get his arms!"

The two men were breathing heavily and, next to him, he heard the man of faith begin to pray again.

"Father, please be with me. O' holy Lord, hallowed be thy name...".

The struggle sounded like it had stopped, and all he could hear now was the snarls, chains clanking, and the men in front of him working to catch their breath.

Then he heard footsteps approach him. They stopped right in front of him, and he felt warm breath hit his cheek.

"You ready for this, boy?" the man asked.

He didn't respond. If they'd given him any water, he might have pissed again, but instead he revealed his fear with a constant shudder and tears.

They removed his blindfold.

Face to face with one of the creatures now, all he could do was scream.

CHAPTER ONE

Lawrence

It was the fourth day that Lawrence Holloway had traveled these roads, and five days since humanity's sudden fall. As much as he wanted to explore and find out what was happening elsewhere, he couldn't bring himself to veer off of this now familiar route. Further keeping him from breaking his habit was the fact that it was raining and he didn't want to get caught in the middle of a bad storm. He made at least one run a day, usually by himself. His goal: to find more people who were alive.

Lawrence had a sort of knack for helping others. In his younger days, he started medical school with high hopes of becoming a surgeon and using his education and gift to help people live better lives. He had always done well in school, and was smart and ambitious. Only a year into the program, however, he got his girlfriend pregnant with their son, forcing Lawrence to drop out of school to support a child. After working a middle-grade office job for about eighteen months, Lawrence decided to enter the medical field as an EMT, later becoming a full-fledged certified paramedic. He loved the job, and continued to study higher levels of medical practice on his own time with hopes of returning to medical school someday to fulfill his dream of becoming a surgeon. Now, as he scanned the desolate highway, he doubted that day would ever come. But, his desire to help people hadn't left him, as he now looked for others to bring into the small community they were building at the hospital.

So far, he had found only four survivors.

There was Trevor, who he actually picked up on the way to the hospital, just hours after everything had gone to hell. Lawrence had been driving down the road in his pickup truck when he came across a man in his 30's struggling with one of the monsters. He'd pulled the car over and, though terribly frightened, jumped out of the vehicle and ran towards the beast with a baseball bat. It had distracted the thing long enough to where Trevor could escape its grasp and look on as Lawrence bashed the thing over the head with the aluminum bat. And he didn't stop at one swing. Lawrence knocked the thing down and continued to attack the monster, even long after it had stopped moving. Blood had shot up from the creature's body, painting Lawrence's powder blue dress shirt a crimson red. Time had slowed down, and after what had seemed to be an hour—he looked back and saw the young man he'd saved looking toward him with a dropped jaw, and eyes wide enough to throw a football through—before Lawrence broke down and started to cry. The young man walked over to try and comfort him, and Lawrence allowed it, though he didn't tell Trevor why he was so distraught.

Then, there were the two women he saved from the accident off of the highway. He'd been driving down I-40, the same path he was taking now, looking for more survivors on the second day. It was his first run since finding refuge at the hospital and had foolishly gone out alone. As he approached a bridge, a van came into view from the on-ramp. He occasionally saw other survivors driving out on the road, but spent most of his time and energy dodging abandoned vehicles and the walking corpses of the sick. Lawrence was about a half mile back from the van when he saw it skid and then flip off the side of the road.

When he reached the van, creatures were already beginning to surround it, and he was forced to act quickly and take them down before they could reach whoever was inside the van. He pulled out the Glock he'd taken off of a fallen police officer, and gunned down the few beasts that were ambling toward the van.

As he checked inside the vehicle for survivors, he found an older woman unconscious behind the wheel, and a younger woman around thirty beginning to stir in the middle row of the van. He called in for back-up and an additional ambulance, and was lucky that no other creatures were in the immediate vicinity.

Their names were Melissa and Jessica, and he hadn't had a lot of time to get to know them yet. Melissa, the older woman, was still unconscious, but she was stable and being looked after at the hospital. The younger girl, Jessica, was awake and responsive, resting easy at the hospital.

Then, just yesterday on another run, Lawrence picked up a man named David, who he found wandering down the side of the road just before he fell into a ditch. At first, Lawrence thought the man might be one of *them*, based on the way he was favoring his left leg when he walked, creating a sort of limp and sway similar to how the creatures moved. Lawrence pulled up close enough to realize that it was, indeed, a man that he saw, and rushed out of the ambulance to the man's side once he saw him fall.

David had acted a little strange ever since Lawrence picked him up, which Lawrence just assumed was because the man was exhausted. The new world had quickly become accustomed to draining people of energy, and even hope, and David looked like he had run out of both.

Unfortunately, Lawrence himself had little to be hopeful for anymore, as well.

***

His most recent run had lasted about an hour and a half. Again, he'd chosen to go alone, a decision that made others in the group uncomfortable. They wanted to help him, but Lawrence was still grieving from things he'd witnessed and done over the past five days, and he used these runs as a type of therapy.

With the hospital in his sight now, Lawrence reached down and grabbed the radio.

"I'm back, over," he said.

"Great, we'll be ready for you." The voice was Sam's, a hospital janitor in his late thirties.

Lawrence pulled through the entrance of the parking garage, where a group of creatures were loitering. He heard their snarls as he drove by, and did his best to avoid eye contact with them as he continued up into the garage and headed for the top level.

He had to climb eight levels to the top level of the parking garage where the group had found a way to block themselves in. They used large boards left over from a construction project to create a barrier between themselves and the creatures. Not many of the creatures loitered there, so the group lived with only minimal worry that the things might be able to bust through and get to them.

"I'm almost there," Lawrence said.

"We hear ya coming," Sam replied.

Lawrence took the final turn around the corner to the eighth level, and he saw three of the creatures walking around near the makeshift gate.

"Can you see how many there are?" Sam asked.

"Just three."

"We'll get 'em."

The large board in the middle moved, and two men came out from behind it and fired at the beasts. It took a few shots, but the three bodies were down and Sam waved Lawrence through the fence.

***

"Thanks, Sam," Lawrence said.

"Don't sweat it, man."

Lawrence shook his hand as Sam clipped the two-way radio back onto his belt. He and Trevor, the man that Lawrence had found on day one of the new world, had been manning the gate to allow Lawrence back inside.

"Find anything?" Sam asked.

Lawrence shook his head.

"Damn."

"I'm gonna go on and head in," Trevor said. Like Sam, he also looked disappointed that Lawrence had come back empty-handed.

Lawrence nodded at him. "Thank you."

Trevor nodded back and then opened the metal access

door into the hospital.

Lawrence grabbed a small duffle bag out of the back of the ambulance, one that he kept some supplies in specifically for runs, and then shut the double doors before turning around to face Sam.

"It's getting worse out there. I saw more of those things, and I only saw a couple of other people driving."

Sam shook his head. "You've got to quit going on those runs by yourself, man."

Lawrence put his hand on Sam's shoulder and patted it. "I know."

And he did know. Lawrence was pushing his luck going out on his own, and knew that it was time for him to do the right thing and quit using the runs as his chance to get lost in his thoughts. There were plenty of places in the wing of the hospital they'd secured where he could be by himself to think.

Lawrence let his arm slip off Sam's shoulder and moved it around the top of his back.

"Come on. Let's head on in."

***

The door from the parking garage led into a narrow access walkway that had windows to the outside. Lawrence tried to avoid looking out, but it was impossible. Every time he walked by, he looked down and saw the creatures limping around the area. Each night stuck in here, he stood on this bridge for at least half an hour, watching the things walk mindlessly around under the light of the moon and the few remaining street lamps. This time, he kept walking, though he still looked down.

At the end of the bridge, they opened another door that led them into the hospital.

Lawrence and Sam entered a corridor with two elevators on each side of the hall. The nurses' station was just past that, and then a collection of rooms down hallways on either side of the desk. The group had isolated themselves in this area of the hospital, which had once housed postpartum care for new mothers and their babies. Now, the area was a refuge for the small group that had managed to get past the first wave of creatures.

"I think that everyone is having an early supper. You gonna join us?" Sam asked.

"Yeah," Lawrence responded. "Let me just get settled in. I wanna wipe myself down and wind down for a few."

"No problem."

Sam headed over to what was once the nurses' break area, and now being used as a kitchen and dining room for these survivors.

Lawrence walked to his room to clean himself up.

***

Lawrence laid the duffle bag down on the bed. He opened it and took inventory of what was there. He still had plenty of ammo for his Glock, the first aid kit was fully stocked with everything he needed, and he still had two full bottles of water.

He sat down on the edge of the bed and placed his hand over his forehead. For the past few days, he'd had headaches on and off that were reaching a near-migraine level of intensity. One was flaring up now, as he could feel the vein on his left temple pulsate under his fingertips.

On the bedside table, there was a small plastic container of ibuprofen that he'd snagged from the medical supply a few doors over, and he popped two of the pills into his mouth, swallowing them without any water. He noticed the 4-by-6 photograph sitting on the table next to it, but ignored it.

Lawrence instead walked over to his table and picked up a bottle of Jack Daniels. He unscrewed the cap and drank straight from the bottle before walking over to the bedside table.

He picked up the picture, taking another swig of the whiskey as he did, the first shot still burning inside his throat. When he turned the photograph over, he began to tear up.

The photograph showed Lawrence with his wife, Bailey, and their son, Carter. The picture was only a few months old, taken at Six Flags Over Georgia. Lawrence was old-fashioned, and still liked collecting printed photographs, even in the digital age. He'd only just recently been convinced by Carter to switch to a digital camera, and bought a nice photo printer so that he could print out photos and still collect the physical prints he was so accustomed to. The photograph he held in his hand was the last one that all three of them had taken together.

Lawrence took another swig of the whiskey before setting the photo back on the bedside table, face down. He stroked it with the back of his hand, as if to try and comfort his family the only way he could now.

"I love you," he mumbled, before he changed into a different t-shirt, and then headed out the door.

CHAPTER TWO

Will

It'd been raining for hours. Driving down Interstate 40 was difficult enough as it was with all the Empties staggering around and all the vehicles left abandoned by their owners, cluttering the path; but trying to navigate through all the obstacles during a downpour proved even more difficult. The past two days had been hell even before the rain, but the group kept on going.

The only thing that Will wanted was to find his mother and father. The group had been trying to reach Knoxville for the past two days, but had only made it just over halfway. They'd gone on and off the interstate, trying to find a back road that might provide a less treacherous path to travel, but they hadn't had any luck. It seemed like every exit they tried, the narrow back roads would be blocked by Empties. After a few attempts, Gabriel convinced Will to just stay on the interstate.

Many times, Will contemplated separating from the group. They were only slowing him down from getting to Knoxville and finding his parents. Between hauling a man recovering from a gunshot wound, a child, and dealing with other people who had their own ideas of what the group should do and where they should go, Will was frustrated. But he knew he couldn't leave Holly and, in the end, he always came back to the same conclusion: *I have a better chance of surviving if I stay with the group.*

They had many confrontations with Empties, which depleted most of their supply of ammunition, and they were now sidetracked again, trying to find somewhere to obtain more bullets for their guns.

"If we run into another large group, we might not make it out. We can't just depend on a baseball bat to kill these things. We've got to find more ammunition, Will," Gabriel said.

Will took his hands off the wheel and put them up. "No shit, dude. Wanna point me to the nearest armory?"

"Quit being an asshole," Gabriel replied.

"Guys!" It was Holly. "Both of you, shut up. Arguing isn't going to do us any good. Let's just chill out, and we'll figure something out. Together."

Both men sighed.

Will gripped the wheel tight, trying to contain his frustration. Everyone in the group was exhausted. They'd fought through horde after horde, and it was taking its toll on all of them, especially Will, Gabriel, and Holly, who were the ones fighting off all the creatures. Marcus was in no position to help, Dylan was just a child, and Miranda didn't know how to use a gun; her medical skills were far too critical to the group's survival for them to put her on the front line anyway.

"Guys, look," Miranda said, pointing down the road.

Will was focused on maneuvering through yet another group of Empties, and hadn't looked far enough down the interstate to see they were fast approaching an exit that had a small shopping center just off of it.

"Try this exit?" Gabriel asked.

Will nodded, and a mile down the road, he took the exit.

***

As they approached the shops, Will had his eye on only one of them.

In between a small convenience store and a discount shoe store, there was a pawn shop. These stores were old and run down, which made them fit perfectly into the new world. He wondered if eventually every building would look like these, or worse. There were Empties in the parking lot, but not more than they could handle. The town looked very small, and the simple shopping center they were approaching might have been the only place for the residents to shop.

"There's no way that place hasn't already been picked apart," Gabriel said of the pawn shop.

Will shrugged. "Maybe. But we've gotta at least check it out."

"Okay, so, what's the plan?"

"It doesn't look too bad. I think you and I can go alone. We'll just take a couple of the handguns. And be sure you've got a knife."

"Fine by me," Gabriel replied. "Pull as close as you can to the door."

There were only about seven Empties in the parking lot, but they all limped toward the SUV as it approached the front door of the pawn shop.

"Holly, can you cover us?" Will asked.

"Of course," Holly replied.

"I can help, too," Marcus added.

"You sure?" Gabriel asked.

Marcus nodded. "I'm feeling a lot better. I got this."

"Alright," Will said. "Just keep these damn things off us. We're gonna be in and out as quick as we can."

"I wanna help," Dylan said from the back of the SUV.

"You can," Gabriel said. "Keep an eye out for any Empties that Holly and Marcus don't see, alright?"

"But I wanna shoot them."

"They need you to watch for others, okay? Can you do that?"

Dylan sighed. "I guess."

"Good," Gabriel said, and then he looked over at Will. "You ready?"

"Are you?" Will replied, smiling.

Gabriel was already opening his door and jumping out of the truck.

***

As Will ran toward the front door of the pawn shop, gunshots behind him halted the snarls that resonated in the air. He looked down and saw an Empty on the ground, which almost looked like it was still twitching from a shot it had just sustained from Gabriel. When Will reached the front door, Gabriel was waiting on him.

"Honors?" Gabriel asked.

Will chuckled and pulled on the door.

Somewhat to his surprise, the door swung open when he pulled the handle. A bell strung to the interior of the door rang once, and Gabriel quickly reached down and muted it with his hand. Will looked back and saw Marcus and Holly with their backs to him, scanning the parking lot with their rifles out the window. Dylan was at the window with his hands pressed against it, looking toward him and Gabriel. Will gave Dylan a thumbs up, then turned around and walked through the door.

***

The little bit of sunlight remaining in the day was the only thing illuminating the inside of the shop. Gabriel still had his gun raised in front of him, but Will had his down at his side. The shop was fairly small and appeared to be vacant, so he didn't see the point in trying to look like an action hero. Will assumed that Gabriel's nerves were calming, because he now lowered his gun as well.

"This is weird," Gabriel said.

"Yeah," Will said, looking around the room.

The shop looked like it hadn't been touched. Aside from the abandoned mechanical garage they stayed in when they escaped from Ellis Metals, everywhere else they'd stopped had been ransacked and beaten to hell. The pawn shop had all its shelves in tact, and the items displayed on the floor were still neatly placed.

A glass case spanned the length of the tiny store. The wall behind it still had some items on the shelves, but much of it was conspicuously empty.

Will walked over to the glass case and saw all the jewelry inside still neatly displayed. As he walked down the length of the case, stroking the glass, he noticed that one part of the case had been emptied. There was nothing left except the price tags in front of where the items had been.

Used Sub Compact .380 Auto - $299

Used Compact Single Action .22 - $229

Used Std. 9mm - $329

“Gabriel,” Will said, waving him over.

Gabriel walked over and looked inside of the case where there had presumably once been guns.

“Shit,” Gabriel said, slamming his fist down on the glass.

Will heard a crash and looked up from the case. A door in the back of the shop swung open, its knob banging against the wall, and a large man appeared in the doorway holding a dual-barrel shotgun. He wore an old, faded yellow t-shirt that had the brand of a pilsner silk-screened across the front, tucked into a pair of pants that were held up by a set of suspenders. He also wore a camouflage trucker hat and had a Fu Manchu mustache. The gun was already pointed toward Will and Gabriel when the man pumped it, preparing the slugs for flight.

“What da fuck y’all doin’ in my shop?”

Gabriel had his gun pointed back at the man, and Will’s hands were up.

“Gabriel, put your gun down,” Will said.

“No fuckin’ way, man.”

“Gabriel!” Will yelled, but Gabriel kept the gun drawn on the hillbilly shop owner.

“I suggest you two pricks get da fuck out here, right now, or y’all both go’na end up dead.”

“We don’t want any trouble,” Will told the man. “We were just coming here looking for ammunition. We’re almost out, and the shop looked abandoned.”

“It look abandoned to you? How da fuck y’all get in here anyways?”

“The door was unlocked, dumb ass,” Gabriel said.

"Gabriel, fucking stop!" Will said.

The man aimed his shotgun right at Gabriel's head. "This dude says some shit like that one more time, I blow both your God damned brains out. Now, I'll say it one more time, get the fuck out of my store, and I'll 'member to lock the God damned door this time."

"Okay, we're leaving," Will said, keeping his hands up and quivering.

"The hell we are!" Gabriel replied.

The bell from the front door rang as it swung open, and the shop owner pointed his gun that way.

Will turned around, his hands still up in the air, and he saw Dylan come walking through the door.

"Dylan!" he cried out. "Get out of here, now!"

But Dylan didn't listen; he stepped all the way through the door.

Will moved, standing between Dylan and the shop owner so that the shotgun was now focused on him instead of at the boy.

"What da fuck is this? How many of you are there?"

"Don't tell him, Will," Gabriel said.

Will ignored him. "The three of us, and there are three more out in our truck."

The man scanned back and forth between Will and Gabriel, and Will could see him swallow hard.

"How many children?"

"Just the one. We also have an injured man. He was shot."

"And y'all been outside trying to survive in all this?"

"Yes. We came from Nashville. We're headed toward

Knoxville. My parents are supposed to be there. We're almost out of ammunition from fighting off hordes of those things outside."

The man still looked back and forth, but Will could tell he was calming a bit. He and Gabriel still had their weapons drawn.

"Please, can we just lower our weapons? We *will* get out of here," Will said.

"Tell your boy here to lower his first."

Will could see the sweat coming off of Gabriel's brow.

"Do it, Gabriel."

Keeping his eyes focused on the man in front of him, Gabriel finally lowered the gun slowly.

"Set it on the glass case next to you," the shop owner commanded in a firm but polite tone.

"Listen to him, Gabe."

Gabriel was clearly frustrated, but he slammed the pistol down onto the glass case and took a few steps away from it.

The shop owner then lowered his shotgun and looked at Will. "What's your name, son?"

"Will." He pointed over his shoulder. "And this is Dylan."

Dylan waved at the man, who smiled down at him.

"Well, Will," the man said, "it's gettin' dark out there. You gonna invite the rest of them folks inside, or not?"

CHAPTER THREE

Jessica

The window inside the hospital room provided the perfect view for watching the sunset. Bedridden by orders of the personnel who remained at the hospital, Jessica took much joy in watching the sun fall behind the horizon both nights she'd been here. The first night, she barely had the energy to keep her eyes open, but had basked in the scene last night. Now, for the third consecutive night, she lay in the bed with nothing to do but gaze out the window, think, and wait.

Jessica didn't look away when a knock came at the door and it swung open.

"Good evening, Ms. Davies," the nurse said.

Jessica kept her focus outside, watching the orange glow slowly fade, only to summon the night to cast its shadow over the small hospital room.

"How does your ankle feel?" the nurse asked.

Finally, Jessica pulled her attention away from the natural spectacle and acknowledged the nurse's presence inside the room. She appeared close to Jessica's age and wore ceil blue scrubs and tennis shoes, her dark blonde hair pulled back into a ponytail.

"It's better," Jessica mumbled.

"And the shoulder?"

Jessica tried to move her shoulder and grimaced.

The nurse made a note on the clipboard she was holding after seeing Jessica's painful reaction. As a result of the van flipping over into the ditch, Jessica had sustained a sprained ankle, some cuts and scratches, and worst of all, had dislocated her right shoulder. Considering how bad the accident had been, she knew her injuries could have been *much* worse. And given just how bad things were outside, she felt like the luckiest woman in the world to now be receiving care from a registered nurse in a somewhat comfortable hospital bed.

Setting down the clipboard, the nurse walked to the end of the bed. She lifted up the covers and unveiled Jessica's bare feet. She reached down and gently squeezed Jessica's injured ankle.

"Does this hurt?"

Jessica shook her head.

"Good. Can you lift your toes toward your head?"

Jessica bent her ankle, pointing her wiggling toes up to her face.

"Perfect," the nurse responded. She picked up the clipboard, jotted down a few notes, and then approached Jessica's side.

The nurse reached over and pressed lightly against Jessica's shoulder, which was in a sling. At the slightest pressure, Jessica grimaced again and reached her opposite hand over to her bad shoulder. The nurse then made a few more notes and crossed her arms.

"Well, the good news is that your ankle seems to be doing a lot better. I think that it's okay to let you walk around some tonight. How's that sound?"

"I'd like that," Jessica said.

"Good. You can come eat with the others. They'd like to meet you. I'll come back in just a few minutes and I can lead you over there."

The young nurse started to turn around, but Jessica stopped her.

"Sarah?"

The blonde woman turned around, smiling. "Yes?"

"How is Mrs. Kessler?"

Sarah frowned, then turned all the way around so that she faced Jessica.

"She's still unconscious, but she's stable. We are taking good care of her."

"When do you think she will wake up?"

Sarah sighed and shook her head. "Don't know. Comas are completely unpredictable. She could wake up tonight, or she could wake up a year from now."

Jessica swallowed, and finally recited the question she'd been scared to ask.

"*Will* she wake up?"

Sarah looked down to the ground for just a moment, before looking back up with an obviously forced smile on her face.

"I think so. Now, get ready to come meet everybody. I'll be back in just a few minutes."

***

Jessica was standing in front of the window staring down into the street, and didn't turn around when Sarah re-entered the room. The sun had gone to sleep, and the scene below was all dark with the exception of a section of sidewalk lit by two lights which, by their dimness, were nearing the end of their kindling. A creature was ambling by, slowly making its way down the dimly lit sidewalk and into the vacant street.

Jessica was still in her gown, but managed to put on a pair of jeans. When she finally turned around, Sarah was smiling at her.

"Guessing it was difficult to put a shirt on?" Sarah asked.

Jessica shrugged. "I didn't even try. Can you help me?"

"Of course."

Sarah walked over and carefully helped Jessica out of the sling. She then untied the simple knot on the gown and pulled it over Jessica's arms. Sarah picked up an oversized t-shirt that she had borrowed from one of the other survivors and carefully led the sleeves over Jessica's arms. Jessica groaned without the support from the sling, but bit down on her lip so to get through it. Once the shirt was over her head and down over her body, Sarah helped her back into the sling and patted her on the back.

"Ready to go eat?" Sarah asked.

Jessica looked into her nurse's eyes. "I want to go see Mrs. Kessler."

"You need to eat, Jessica. And Mrs. Kessler ne—"

"Please."

Sarah sighed and nodded toward the door. "Come on."

***

The room was in the same hallway as Jessica's, five doors down to be exact. The door was closed all the way and, as Sarah opened it, Jessica could hear the heavy breathing and the clicks of the machinery around Melissa, all doing its part to keep her stable.

Sarah stopped just as she opened the door about halfway. "Are you ready?"

Jessica took a deep breath and then nodded.

Sarah opened the door the rest of the way and stood with her back against it, clearing a path for Jessica to look down at Melissa on the bed.

She lay there on her back, facing the pale ceiling above. There were lights mounted to the wall above the headboard on either side of the bed, both powered on and shining just enough for Jessica to see her. Melissa's eyes were closed, and an oxygen mask over her face helped keep her breathe steady. A blanket covered her all the way up to just below her neckline, and Jessica could see she was wearing a similar gown to the one she herself had been wearing. Melissa's chest rose and fell every few seconds, almost in the same rhythm as the machines around her. Her face looked older than it had before, as if the accident had drawn ten years out of her life in one instant.

Jessica moved to the side of the bed and the hurt rose up inside of her. She covered her mouth to muffle the initial sob and started to cry. She'd only known Melissa for a few days, but felt like she'd been through a lifetime with her. Jessica had been saved by the woman's husband, Walt, and then was there with Melissa when he turned into one of *them*. Similarly, Melissa had comforted Jessica after she walked into her parents' bedroom only to see them dead of self-inflicted gunshot wounds. Jessica and Melissa had been through a lot together, and now the older woman was clinging onto her life right before Jessica's eyes.

Sarah stepped into the room behind Jessica and began to rub her hands over her back.

"She seems strong," Sarah said. "I think she'll get better."

Jessica just continued to cry.

"Here, let's sit down, sweetie," Sarah suggested. She led Jessica over to a pair of chairs, and they both took a seat.

"Have you known her a long time?" Sarah asked.

Jessica sniffled and shook her head. "Just a few days."

"Oh. Did you meet... *after?"*

Jessica nodded. "I work in...*worked* in a hotel in the mountains, kinda near Asheville." She tilted her head toward Melissa. "She and her husband had just checked in that day." Jessica really wasn't in the mood to talk about any of this at the moment with this stranger, and realized her mistake right after mentioning Walt, and predicted the question that would follow.

"Husband?" Sarah asked. "Where is he now?"

Jessica looked toward the wall for a moment before taking a deep breath and looking back to the nurse. "He didn't make it."

"I'm sorry," Sarah said.

"It's okay, I just really don't want to talk about this right now. Can we just go eat?"

Sarah nodded and put her arm around Jessica. "Come on, let's go."

They both stood, and Jessica walked over to the side of the bed. She grabbed Melissa's hand and held onto it for a moment.

"I'll come back and see you later," she whispered. "Just rest."

She gently set Melissa's hand back down, and then turned around and made her way out of the room with Sarah.

***

"How's it feel walking on that ankle?" Sarah asked.

Jessica was looking down toward her feet as she limped down the hallway. "It's okay. I think it'll be better once my lower body wakes up a little bit. Laying in that bed the past couple of days hasn't done a whole lot for my lower back."

Sarah smiled. "That'll all subside, I promise."

Just past where Jessica's room was, a door was open to one of the other rooms. As they passed by the door, Sarah stopped and looked inside. There was a man sitting on the bed, and Jessica made eye contact with him for just a moment. He was a good-looking man, a bit older than her, and didn't look like he had worked at the hospital.

"Everything okay in there, Mr. Ellis?" Sarah asked with a smile.

The man nodded and waved. "Just fine."

"Will you be joining us for dinner?"

"Maybe in a little while," Ellis replied. "I'm not really hungry right now."

"Alright. Well, we'll be eating in the lounge if you want to join us."

Jessica made eye contact with him again, and smiled. He curved his mouth slightly, and then looked back down at his hands.

"You mind shutting that door?" he asked politely.

"No problem. Just buzz if you need anything, okay, David?"

"Thank you," he said, and the two women continued their

slow trek to the break room.

As they walked away from the room, Jessica turned to Sarah and asked, "What happened to him?"

Sarah shrugged. "We aren't really sure yet. He hasn't said much. Lawrence found him in a ditch on the side of the interstate. We think he may have a concussion, but he has been pretty vague about where he was before here. Not sure if he remembers, to be honest."

"Oh, my God."

"Yeah. He's lucky that Lawrence was there, or he for sure would have been killed by those things outside."

Jessica thought back to all the creatures they saw during their trip that led them here, and wondered if the nurse had any concept of just how bad it was out there.

Sarah smiled. "Come on, the lounge is just over here."

***

As they approached the room, Jessica could hear light chatter coming from inside. Sarah had told her that they were headed to the nurses' break room and lounge. It was behind a door that required a key card to open it and had a sign on the door that read "Staff Only".

Jessica walked into the room, and saw four people were sitting inside: two women and two men. The room featured a countertop with a microwave, a small sink, a refrigerator, a sofa and love seat, and a large table in the middle of the room where the four survivors were eating. Three of them had plates in front of them with only scraps left on them, and the other—one of the women, a nurse who'd treated Jessica some since she arrived at the hospital—was still working on her dinner. Inside, Jessica was elated. They'd fed her well since she'd been bedridden in the hospital, but it felt like years since she last sat down at a table and had a real meal with other people.

The group stopped talking and stared at Jessica. Sarah stepped into the room, smiling.

"Guys, this is Jessica Davies," Sarah said. She looked over to Jessica. "You've already met Kristen." She was the other nurse who had tended to Jessica.

"This here is Brandon; he's an anesthesiologist."

"Good to see you up and walking," Brandon said.

Sarah pointed to the other woman. "This is Rachel. She is an administrator here."

Rachel raised her glass of water toward Jessica.

"And finally, this is Trevor. Lawrence found Trevor out there just like he found you and Mrs. Kessler."

Trevor smiled and nodded at Jessica. "Hi," he said timidly.

Sarah walked over to a counter on the other side of the room. "You can grab you a plate right here. We've got salad, some chicken, a few different veggies, and some fruit. Grab what you want."

"Thank you," Jessica mumbled, and she limped over to the counter and fixed herself a plate.

As she sat down at the table, she looked over and saw Lawrence walk into the room. He was wearing a red plaid shirt tucked into a pair of jeans. He noticed Jessica and raised his eyebrows.

"Well, very nice to see you, Jessica."

Jessica nodded and smiled.

"She walked in here herself without any help," Sarah said.

Lawrence put his hands on his waist and nodded. "Excellent. Glad to see that you're doing better."

Jessica turned from him and grabbed a fork with the hand on her left arm, her good arm. She was right-handed, so eating would take a little bit more effort than normal, but she was so hungry that she didn't care.

"Did you find anyone else?" Kristen asked Lawrence.

Jessica turned to see him shaking his head.

"I know you're tired of hearing this and I know that you're still hurting from what happened, but you've got to take one of us with you when you go out there," Brandon told Lawrence. "It's too dangerous for you to be going alone. Hell, you almost got yourself killed when you found Jessica, here."

Lawrence sighed. "I know."

"I'll go," Rachel said. "I wanna see what it's like out there."

"No you don't," Jessica mumbled before Lawrence could answer. She looked around the room and everyone was just staring at her. She cleared her throat and took a sip of the water in front of her. "You've got a good thing here. Enjoy it. You don't want to go out there."

Rachel looked frustrated and was about to speak, but Trevor butted in.

"She's right," he said. "You don't want to go out there."

"They are right, Rachel," Lawrence added.

Rachel put down her fork and stood up. "Okay, then. Guess I'll just go back to my fucking desk and wait for the phone to ring, how about that?"

She stormed out of the room before anyone could stop her.

Jessica looked up at Lawrence. “Sorry.”

Lawrence smiled and patted her on her good shoulder. “It’s fine. She’s just getting a little bit of cabin fever and she doesn’t understand. Go on and finish your dinner. You’ve got to be starving.”

She was, and she went back to scarfing down the food in front of her.

CHAPTER FOUR

David

David Ellis sat at the edge of the bed, staring down at the floor. Before Lawrence and the girl stopped by the room, a nurse came in and suggested that he lie back down and rest. He ignored her, and instead chose to sit up. He'd been lying down in that bed since the moment he arrived the previous day, and he was becoming antsy.

He felt the urge in his bladder to use the restroom, and walked to the toilet.

The bathroom inside the hospital room was simple. It had only a toilet and a sink, which had a very small vanity in front of it as well as a mirror plastered to the wall above it. David pulled down his pants and closed his eyes as he urinated, feeling the pang in his gut begin to fade away. The luxury of having indoor plumbing was one he hadn't been sure he'd ever know again, and he was pleased to be experiencing it here after two days of hell out on the road.

When he was done, he flushed the toilet, and then looked at himself in the mirror. He had on a gown, which he was already tired of. He didn't care for the tickle of the open air hitting his bare backside. His curly hair looked like he'd just woken up from a week-long nap, and the stubble on his face looked like it had increased ten-fold overnight.

On a table near his bed, there was a fresh set of clothes

for him. On top, there was a note that read: "Hope these fit. Had to guess on the size. Not too many options. - L". David stared at the clothes after he was done reading the note, and slipped out of the gown. The pants fit just about right, while the shirt was a little tight, but he was okay with it. His toned biceps strained the short sleeves of the shirt, and it felt great to wear a fresh pair of underwear.

While he wasn't hungry, David was going to go stir crazy if he stayed in the room any longer. He figured that, with everyone presumably at dinner, it'd be a good time to go have a look around.

So, that's exactly what he planned to do as he opened the door and stepped out into the hallway.

***

He looked both ways after he stepped out of the room, and saw that it was clear in both directions. He quietly pulled the door shut behind him, so as to not catch the attention of anyone who might be lurking around. David could hear the chatter down the hallway, presumably coming from where the group was eating dinner, so he headed the opposite direction. They'd kept David in his room since he arrived here the day before, and he was curious to learn more about where the stranger had brought him.

Either side of the hallway was lined with doors, each one numbered with a small metal plate, just like the room he was staying in. Most of them were open and didn't appear to have anyone occupying them. Two of the open rooms he passed did have belongings in them, proving to David that other people were in fact living in at least some of these hospital beds.

When he reached the end of the hall, he looked to to one side and noticed a pair of double doors just a few steps around the corner. To the other, there was a set of elevators at the dead end of the hall, also just a few yards from where he was standing. He stepped toward the elevators and read the signs taped to the metal doors that read “Do Not Use”.

He started to turn around, and he heard someone walking down the hall from the direction he’d come, mumbling as they moved swiftly. David stepped back and stood with his back against the elevator, with the frame of the door hopefully hiding just enough of him to where he wouldn’t be noticed.

A woman appeared from around the corner, heading toward the double doors. She had a clipboard in her hand and was shaking her head as she walked, still grumping indistinctly to herself. David watched her as she pushed hard through the double doors, hearing them crash into the walls as they swung in.

At the end of another short hallway, the woman headed around a corner, disappearing from David’s vision.

He stepped away from the elevators and followed.

***

The hallway was only dimly lit. A sign on the double doors read “Employees Only” written on notebook paper with a black marker and then taped on with Scotch tape. He ignored it, curious to know where the frustrated woman was headed.

At the end of the room, he turned the same direction the woman had, and walked down the lengthy corridor.

On either side of him, there were closed doors. It looked

very similar to the area he was staying in, only this part of the hospital was dark and cold. He opened a couple of the doors and noticed that they were simply abandoned hospital exam rooms. The two rooms looked identical, both containing the uncomfortable, table-like bed you'd sit on if you were a patient, the doctor's small rolling stool, a sink, and a small cabinet.

At the end of the hall, he could only go left, which put him in another hallway. This time, though, he could see a glowing light at the end.

David crept down the hall, and as he made it near the end, he heard the woman scratching notes onto the clipboard while still mumbling to herself. He stood with his back against a door that was slightly ajar, and listened.

"They send me here to deal with this shit, but they don't trust me to go outside," the woman said, then sighed. "Such bullshit."

She continued to mumble to herself, and David stepped out of the doorway and peeked around the corner.

The woman was standing there, as he'd imagined her, looking through a window and jotting down notes on the clipboard.

David narrowed his eyes when he heard something else. A faint sound was coming from near the woman, though he couldn't make out what exactly it was.

The woman sighed again and then reached up and hung the clipboard on the wall in front of her.

David backed up around the corner, ducking into an open room just as the woman stepped away from the window and headed toward him.

From inside the room, he watched her walk away through the crack in the door.

David counted to twenty, then poked his head out of the room.

He looked out and saw that no one was coming or going, so he stepped out into the hallway. The noise he heard earlier became more distinct. Along with a low hiss, there was a repeated clatter.

His bare feet moved gently over the floor as he headed around the corner toward the lit room the woman had been standing in front of.

And as he approached the window and looked inside the room, his eyes went wide.

“Holy shit.”

All he could do was stare at it. The room appeared to have once been a gift shop, its contents pulled out so that the room was empty except for a bed, a small table, and some sort of machine. The thing was strapped into the bed, chomping its jaws and trying to break loose as it spit and hissed into the air. There were cords coming off of its body, hooked up to various machines. David looked at the clipboard, which had various numbers scribbled next to acronyms and initials that he couldn’t translate.

He stood there watching the Empty squirm and try to break free for what seemed like an hour.

“Amazing, isn’t it?”

David jumped when the man’s deep voice came from his left, and his dark shadow loomed in the bits of light. As a reflex, he reached to his pants for a knife that wasn’t there. If it had been, the man in the shadow would have been dead.

Lawrence approached David, smiling and looking into the room.

"Her name is Joanne. She was a patient here when everything happened."

David sighed and narrowed his eyes at the man. "You scared the shit out of me."

"Sorry."

David shook his head, then glared at it. "Why is it here?"

Lawrence looked over at David. "See, we got lucky. This woman was actually a very bad person. She was a criminal, a drug dealer. She had OD'd, and they had her strapped in so that, when she came to, she wouldn't be able to escape and the police could arrest her. There was so much going on up here after everyone fell, that she was basically forgotten about. So, she remained unscathed. Once the rest of the area had been cleared out, Kristen—one of the nurses who is still here now—left her in her room and shut the door. When I got here, they wanted me to go in and kill her, but I figured we oughta keep her alive. Study her. So, we cleared out this gift shop and put her in here so we could look in on her through this large window."

"Shit," David said. "Have you found out anything?"

Lawrence raised his eyebrows and put his hands in his pockets, bouncing up and down on his toes. "Unfortunately, I'm not a doctor. While I have studied to become one, there are only so many things I know to do. The only thing we know for certain is that it's not viral. We ran some tests, but couldn't find any kind of strain. Other than that, we honestly don't know much."

David rubbed the stubble on his chin, and the creature

made eye contact with him. He wondered if it actually knew that he was standing there, or what he even was. He'd assumed that whatever had caused everyone to change was viral, and was perplexed to find otherwise.

In regards to Lawrence, David was starting to see *some* value in him. The man was learning things about these new beings, and David decided it best to lay low and play along, at least for the time being. As hungry as he was to be in control and to obtain power in the new world, he knew that he first needed to survive, and blending in and understanding these monsters would go a long way toward reaching that goal.

"You can't tell the others that you were here. Not everyone knows Joanne is here."

David nodded.

"Can I walk you back to your room?" Lawrence asked.

"Sure," David said, and the two men stepped away from the glass as the thing's snarls faded behind them.

CHAPTER FIVE

Will

"Thank you for inviting us in here, Donny."

"Don't mention it."

Will looked over at Gabriel, who was standing at the other end of the room, and then back to the shop owner. "And sorry my guy went all cowboy on you."

Donny, the store owner, spit his dip into a plastic bottle, then said, "It's okay. The way things been goin', made folks a wee bit crazy. I understand. Hard to trust others."

Donny had taken the group into a cellar located under the shop. There was a back room with a door in the floor that led down to it. Will was now sitting next to him with his back against a wall.

"He's got a wife and kid in D.C. he's had trouble getting in contact with. He's pretty high strung, as you might imagine. You got any kids? A wife?"

Donny removed his cap and wiped his brow. He had his elbows over his knees, and his gut protruded further over his waistband because of how he was sitting. He put his cap back on, and then looked over toward Dylan. The boy had finished eating his portion of the canned soup that Donny had shared with the group, and was now sitting with Holly playing a game of Connect Four that Donny had had for sale in the shop above them.

"Cathy, my wife, she died four years ago. The cancer got her. And my daughter, she was fourteen. She got caught up in all this shit a few days back." He began to cry now. "I left her in the double-wide we were livin' in. She attacked me, but I couldn't bring myself to put 'er down. She's still locked up in there now, I 'magine."

Will shook his head and put his hand over his eyes. "I'm so sorry, man."

"Yeah." It's the only response that Donny could muster up. He changed the subject. "So, y'all headed to Knoxville?"

Will nodded. "Hoping to find my mom and dad there."

"Then what?"

Will gave him a confused look.

"Where you gonna go after that?" Donny asked.

Will sighed and looked over to Gabriel again. "I imagine we'll head toward the East Coast. See if maybe we can't get Gabriel and Dylan back to their families."

Donny shook his head. "That's an awful long way to go."

Will shrugged. "Not quite sure where else we'd go. Hoping maybe they've set up some kind of refuge out there. Or, at least, maybe that they have one planned. What about you? You just gonna stay here?"

"Don't really see any reason to leave. I've got protection, shelter, food to last me a while. It's pretty safe here."

"As long as you lock the door," Will said with a smile, and both men laughed.

The others in the room were talking amongst each other, while eating canned food that Donny had given them. He had a large supply of it down in this cellar, along with lots of bottled water and plenty of weapons that he collected through the pawn shop. Will wondered if Donny was one of those survivalist types that was always Doomsday prepping, but he didn't bother asking. He was just thankful that the man had invited him and the group inside.

Gabriel stood up with his empty can and made his way over to where Will and Donny were sitting. He had a sour look on his face, but he reached his hand out to Donny, who took it and shook.

"Thank you," Gabriel said, "for bringing us in. And, I'm sorry."

Donny smiled, letting go of Gabriel's hand. "It's alright. I pointed my gun first. Besides, your boy here filled me in on some of the shit ya got goin' on. Sorry to hear 'bout all that."

Gabriel acknowledged the shop owner's sentiment with a nod, then turned back around and walked over to where Holly and Dylan were sitting.

Will yawned and stretched his arms up over his head.

"You look exhausted," Donny said.

"Just a little."

"Get ya some rest."

"Thank you for all this."

"Don't mention it. Now, seriously, get ya some sleep, friend."

Will curled up on the floor where he sat. Compared to being stuffed in the car with five other people, the hard floor of the cellar with the single, thin blanket under him felt like a suite at the Hilton. And within minutes, he was fast asleep.

***

Gabriel

When Gabriel awoke the next morning, he noticed that

Dylan was no longer beside him. The boy had fallen asleep right next to him, but now he was gone.

Gabriel stood up and scanned the room. Everyone else was still fast asleep on the cellar floor, except Donny, who had a small cot that he slept in. The shop owner had offered to sleep on the floor so that Dylan or one of the women could use the cot, but each had respectfully declined, understanding that they were in his space. Stepping over bodies, Gabriel headed for the steps that led up into the shop.

Once he reached the top, he looked out through the open door that led out into the main part of the shop. Empty cardboard boxes and shelves filled with pawned items that people hadn't picked up yet—and likely, never would—cluttered the storage room, but there was just enough space left around the door to walk in and out of it. Through the open door, Gabriel could see that Dylan was sitting near the front of the store, looking out into the world through the large glass window. The sun wasn't quite up yet, so only a little bit of light was shining into the building. Gabriel stepped into the main part of the shop and slowly made his way toward Dylan, rubbing his eyes as he tried to wake up.

Dylan kept his eyes focused on the outside world as Gabriel approached him. He was yawning, and his bare feet slapped against the tiled floor as he came up to the boy. In addition, he was still wearing the pair of track pants he lifted from the sporting goods store, and they swished as they rubbed together with each step he took. He wasn't wearing a shirt, and could smell the foul odor coming off of his unbathed body, an odor that he hadn't yet gotten used to.

There was no doubt Dylan both heard and smelled him, but nevertheless, his eyes remained fixed on the parking lot.

When he reached Dylan, he stood at his side and the boy finally acknowledged him with a quick glance, before looking back outside. Gabriel sighed, then looked out the window as well. In the distance, he could see the orange glow beginning to appear over the horizon, and the clouds were ringed in a dark grey, signaling the distinct possibility of more rain. The truck still sat outside, unscathed, and there were no Empties around. Gabriel had worried about leaving the truck out in the open, but with no access from behind the building to hide it, they hadn't had a choice.

Gabriel waited for the boy to speak, but when the moment never came, he spoke first.

"Sleep alright?"

Dylan shrugged, looking down at the ground for a moment before looking back outside.

Gabriel sat down next to Dylan with his knees up and his elbows folded over them.

"What's on your mind, bud?"

Dylan remained silent. Gabriel could tell the boy was thinking about something. The young kid was giving off the same vibe that Gabriel's daughter would when she was only pretending she didn't want him to ask what was going on with her. Gabriel had played this game before.

Gabriel started to stand. "Alright, guess I'll leave you alone and let you be to yourself."

Dylan sighed, then finally spoke. "I'm not sure I want to go home."

Gabriel cracked a small smile, almost laughing at his

successful tactic that had gotten the boy to speak, but then let settle in what the boy had said, and wiped the smile from his face. He sat back in the same position, with his arms propped over his raised knees.

"And why wouldn't you want that?"

The boy looked down to the floor and mumbled, "I like you guys better."

"But, Dylan, they are your parents. I'm sure that, somewhere out there, likely at home, they are missing the heck out of you. Just like I miss my own daughter."

"Yeah, but, you *love* her."

"Yes, yes, I do. And, I'm sure that your parents love you."

"I don't think so." Dylan was still looking down at the ground, as if he were embarrassed.

Right as Gabriel was about to continue the conversation, he heard the sound of footsteps coming up the steps behind him, followed by a familiar, sweet voice.

"Hey, Gabe, we need you down here," Holly said.

Gabriel looked back. "Be there in a minute."

"Okay. Try to hurry. We've got breakfast, too, so bring Dylan."

Gabriel looked down at Dylan. "Why don't you come get some breakfast? That might make you feel a little better."

Dylan sighed, and slowly nodded. "Yeah, okay, I guess."

Gabriel stood, then reached down and took the boy's hand, helping him up. He wrapped his arm around Dylan as they headed for the stairs.

***

After he finished his canned soup breakfast, Gabriel felt a tap on his shoulder. He turned around, and Will was moving to his side, kneeling down.

"Hey, Donny wants to talk to us upstairs real quick," Will said.

"Alright." Gabriel sat down his empty bowl and stood up.

He followed Will up the stairs, leaving the rest of the group behind to finish their meals, basking in the fact that they weren't crammed together in a vehicle and could stretch their legs out.

Donny was in the main part of the shop waiting on the men when they reached the top of the stairs. Will walked over to him first and Gabriel followed close behind. The large man sighed and put his hands on his hips.

"I 'preciate you folks givin' me some company," Donny said.

"We can't thank you enough for letting us stay here," Will replied.

Donny nodded. "Well, I'm afraid it's time for you to go. I ain't tryin' to be rude or nothin', I just gotta protect my resources and be stingy with 'em, if ya know what I mean."

"We completely understand," Will said. "We just appreciate you giving us a roof for one night and some food, especially after the way we barged in here."

Donny turned his attention to Gabriel. "Yeah, well, sorry it had to be like that."

Gabriel nodded at the man, acknowledging he felt the same way. He knew that, if he were in the same position as the shop owner, he would have acted the exact same way and done what he could to protect what was his.

"Well, I don't want you folks to leave empty-handed and such," Donny said.

The man pulled up his pants and walked back into the storage room. When he came back out a few moments later, he had a filing box filled with packs of ammunition.

"I saw what y'all were packin'. This should help y'all squeeze by a little bit longer."

"Are you sure?" Will asked.

Donny looked at Gabriel and chuckled. "Consider this my apology."

Gabriel smiled. "Accepted." He grabbed the box.

"I also want y'all to take some of that there food I got down there. You got a child with ya, and I couldn't let ya leave knowin' that boy may not eat for a while."

"Thank you so much," Will said.

Donny tipped his hat and leaned up against the wall. "Ya know, I don't see people in this world bein' too nice anymore. It's good to at least see there's still at least a few of ya out there."

He extended his hand out to Gabriel, who shook it and gave the man a nod of respect. Donny repeated the same act with Will.

"Alright, now let's go wrangle up some food for y'all and getcha on your way."

CHAPTER SIX

Lawrence

Lawrence was the first one walking the hallways in the morning. At least, he hadn't seen anyone else yet. He kept the lights off to conserve precious power, knowing that electricity may not be a long-term guarantee, and walked the dim hallways. He went to the break room first thing to make a pot of coffee, and as he walked down the hallway, he savored every sip of the black gold, not knowing how long he'd be afforded the luxury of morning brew. Nothing was guaranteed in this world anymore, especially something as trivial as coffee.

He decided to go check on the unconscious woman that he'd rescued a few days prior with the young girl, Jessica. While Jessica hadn't taken the time to get to know the group yet, he could see potential in her from the little bit of conversation they'd had, and felt she could be a valuable part of their team at the hospital. But, he also knew she wasn't going to be of much use until Melissa was awake and feeling better.

The door to Melissa's room was closed, but he turned the handle and it swung open. Lawrence was surprised to see two people inside the small room. Melissa was on the bed, still breathing through the power of the machine hooked up to her. She was facing the ceiling, as her chest rose and fell gently, over and over.

The room had an uncomfortable sofa that was built into the frame below the exterior window, and Jessica was lying on it, curled up and fast asleep.

Lawrence smiled, and had started to turn back out of the room when he heard the young girl begin to stir on the couch. He watched Jessica open her eyes and look over at him.

"Good morning," Lawrence said.

"Hey," Jessica said, stretching and yawning simultaneously.

"Can't think that you slept too well on that thing."

Jessica chuckled. "Yeah, well, I didn't want to leave her."

"Understood."

"Did you come to check on her?"

Lawrence nodded and walked over to Melissa. He grabbed a clipboard from Melissa's bedside table and jotted down a few readings from the machines hooked up to her.

"How is she?" Jessica asked.

"Stable. She's about the same. Did she move at all during the night?"

Jessica shook her head. "Well, she kind of started to, but I realized it was nothing. She sort of... twitched for a moment, before she was still again."

Lawrence nodded, and wrote down another note concerning what Jessica had just told him.

"Do you think she will come out of this soon?" Jessica asked.

"I'm just a paramedic, not a doctor. I don't even try to predict these types of things. She could come out of it tomorrow, or she could come out of it next year. We really don't know."

Jessica looked down to the ground. "Yeah, that's what the nurse said."

"I'm sorry." He scratched his chin, then put the clipboard back on the table. "How do you know her, anyways? You don't really look alike, so I'm assuming you aren't related."

Lawrence listened as Jessica told him about the hotel, the gas station, and finally, her parents' house. It took almost ten minutes for her to tell the whole story, but when she was done, Lawrence stood silent for a few moments.

"I'm so sorry," he said.

"Yeah," Jessica replied simply.

"Well, we are going to do everything we can for her, okay?"

"Okay," Jessica mumbled, and from her stoic face, Lawrence couldn't tell if she actually believed him.

Lawrence looked down at his watch. "They should be getting breakfast ready about now. You should go."

"Yeah, maybe I will."

"Good. I'll come back and check on y'all in a bit, alright?"

Jessica nodded and sat up straight on the couch as Lawrence turned and left the room.

***

David

With every repetition, the sweat dripped off David Ellis' forehead and onto the ground. He was beginning to feel normal again and was quickly adjusting to life inside the secure hospital. He had been anxious to get back to his morning exercise regimen, and with each push-up, his biceps ached as they worked to readjust to the strain of the movement.

After seventy-five push-ups, he flipped onto his back and began to do some bicycle crunches. Inside his body, he still held several pints of anger over what had happened inside his building in Nashville, and he was especially pissed off by how Marcus had betrayed him. He'd seen the man as both a good friend and one of his company's best employees, and couldn't believe that Marcus hadn't understood his vision of keeping everyone alive. He could even still feel the pain in his neck from where he'd been struck with the baseball bat. Almost as fast as the world had changed, David's little dream community had fallen, and he was now alone with a bunch of strangers who knew nothing of his history or of what he planned to do.

The door opened as he panted, his heart rate soaring and his obliques burning.

Lawrence appeared in the doorway, shutting the door behind him as he entered the room. Though David had noticed the man enter out of the corner of his eye, he didn't look his way to acknowledge he was there. Instead, he continued his exercise.

"I see you're getting back to normal," Lawrence said.

Counting to himself, David finally stopped the bicycle crunches, and lay flat on his back, placing his hands over his quickly rising and falling stomach.

"That's good to see. We could use some more muscle around here."

Having finished his exercises and recovered enough to stand, David looked over to Lawrence and jumped to his feet.

He grabbed a towel and wiped himself down, starting with his bare chest and his stomach, then under his arms, and then finally his face with the opposite side of the towel.

When he pulled the towel from in front of his eyes, he saw Lawrence staring down at his stomach. David looked down and remembered the scars on his body, and quickly grabbed a t-shirt off of the bed and pulled it over his head, hoping to avoid the man asking him about his markings.

"Strength coming back?" Lawrence asked.

"Getting there."

"Good. I'd like to take you on a run with me."

David grabbed the towel again and ran it through his hair. He'd been stuck in this hospital room too long, and the thought of getting the hell out was appealing. "Okay, when?"

Lawrence looked down at his watch. "I was hoping we could leave in about twenty minutes."

David pointed to the watch on the man's wrist. "What you gonna do when that battery runs out?"

Lawrence laughed and shook his head. "Twenty minutes?"

David nodded, and Lawrence turned around and left the room.

***

It was more like thirty-five minutes when the two men were finally in the ambulance, heading down the swirled parking garage. David looked around, expecting to see Empties, but there were none inside the garage.

"They ever get in here?" he asked.

"Occasionally," Lawrence said. "Of course we have that barrier at the top of the garage. They haven't made it through that yet, and hopefully it stays that way."

Moments later, they were speeding out of the garage, and David finally saw the Empties he'd expected to see on the way down through the parking garage. The sun had made its way up from behind the horizon for the first time in the past couple of days. It had been raining, but the sun was out and warmed the slightly chilled autumn air.

They passed a sign that said "To I-40 West", and David looked over to Lawrence.

"Where we headed?"

"Going to try and find more survivors."

"Why?"

Lawrence looked over at him and smiled. "Why? Why not?"

"You've got a good thing going back there at that hospital. Electricity, plenty of resources for the group that's already there to survive. Why risk it by bringing in more people to use those resources? And what if you come across a sour grape who has a different plan than you do for survival?"

For a few moments, Lawrence was quiet. He concentrated on pulling out onto the interstate before he replied.

"We have to show that there's still good people in the world. That we can survive, together... persevere."

"And what if there aren't any good people anymore?" David asked.

Lawrence traded glances between David and the road. "You trying to tell me something?"

"No," David lied, knowing inside that *he* was one of the bad ones. "Just trying to make you realize what you have. It's hell out here."

"And that's why we have to help people," Lawrence said.

David stared outside and didn't respond. They were passing through an industrial part of town and he saw a line of warehouses, similar to where he'd spent his first couple of days in the new world. For a moment, he wondered if there were survivors in any of those buildings, but then he looked back out at the road. He considered the man sitting next to him. The group at the hospital had it good, much better than he assumed most people had it out here in this godforsaken world. How could the man be looking to invite more and more people in? With the resources they had at the hospital, the small group who was already there could endure for a long time with little need to go out into the world.

And with that, David decided: the group was going to need a new leader. Someone else needed to be making decisions.

Lawrence Holloway was weak, and he needed to go.

CHAPTER SEVEN

Will

The sun was out, which, in and of itself, put a smile on Will's face as the group pulled away from the pawn shop.

Will sat in the very back of the SUV, cuddled up to Holly. He'd decided to let Gabriel take the first shift driving, which he hoped would be the only shift necessary between here and Knoxville. Dylan sat in the front seat with Gabriel, and Miranda was redressing Marcus' wound on the middle seat just in front of Will.

"You feeling better?" Holly asked Marcus.

He turned his head to the side and glanced back at her. "Yeah. It sure was nice to stay the night under a roof and be able to really stretch out."

"No shit," Will said.

Marcus smiled for a moment before grimacing and clutching his shoulder.

"Sorry," Miranda said.

"Damn. Go easy," Marcus told her.

Miranda smiled, shaking her head, and continued to work on covering the gunshot back up.

Holly rested her head against Will's chest, and he ran his fingers through her hair. The two had become very close over the last few days, though they hadn't actually had any time alone together. Will hoped that would change soon, as he wanted to be able to sit down with the girl and have an actual conversation without the others around. With the way things were going, he wasn't sure when or if he'd have that opportunity.

"We're going to get there today," Holly said.

"I hope so. A three-hour trip has taken us three days."

"And we're going to find your parents. I know they're there, Will. And that they're safe. I can just feel it."

Will continued to run his fingers through Holly's hair, and he leaned his head back against the seat and shut his eyes.

"Yeah. Yeah, I hope so."

The truth was, Will had begun to lose hope that he'd ever see his parents again. He wondered if the people around him would be the only family he'd have from here on out. He still had *some* hope, from the text message he received, but it was quickly fading. Added to that was the fact that every time he tried to call the number back, he got nothing more than a busy signal. Most times, though, the line was silent. Both his patience and his faith were wearing thin, fast.

"I just want to meet them to tell you how much of a gallant hero you are," Holly said, smirking at him.

"Hahaha," Will replied.

Marcus turned around and looked at him.

"Hey, man, don't underestimate what you did back there for us. That was some serious shit."

Will laughed. "Dude, I was kidnapped. Not like I had much of a choice."

"The hell you didn't!" Marcus said. He turned all the way around so that he could look directly at Will. "You could have kept driving when she waved at you." Marcus nodded toward Holly, and Will looked at her. "But, you didn't. You came to help her. Plus, you're a smart dude, man. You probably could have gotten away if you really wanted to before you came to save my sorry ass.

"Either way, the point is you didn't. You helped us. And now, here we are."

"Yeah, but, what is *here?"* Will asked.

"Here is a hell of a lot better than back there," Miranda said.

Holly looked up and kissed Will on his cheek, then looked him in the eyes. "It's much better. We're going to be fine."

***

Gabriel

For once, the road ahead was fairly clear. While there were some Empties and abandoned cars out on the highway, most of the vehicles had gone off of the road, making it much easier to maneuver. He hoped that this would be the day they finally reached Knoxville, so they could find Will's parents, and head on toward the East Coast.

At the same time, Gabriel had other things on his mind.

Ever since their talk earlier that morning, Dylan had been acting strange. He sat in the front passenger seat while Gabriel drove, but had yet to say a single word. While he wanted to continue their conversation, Gabriel really wasn't sure if this was the time or the place, not with the others around.

When he looked over to Dylan, the boy was tossing a small, red rubber ball that Donny gave to him. The kid looked as if he was focusing intently, and Gabriel wondered what the boy was thinking.

Soon after, he stopped tossing the ball, and Gabriel didn't have to wonder anymore.

"Why are they here?" Dylan asked.

The four that sat behind Gabriel and the boy stopped talking, and Gabriel could see in the rearview mirror that they were looking up toward Dylan now.

"Why are *who* here?" Gabriel asked the boy.

Out of the corner of his eye, Gabriel could see Dylan finally look up at him, and he glanced over at him while trying to keep an eye on the surprisingly open road.

Dylan pointed to Gabriel's left, and Gabriel looked out of the driver's side window.

They were passing a vast, wide-open corn field. It seemed to go on forever until it finally met the slowly rising sun at the horizon. About fifty yards off the road, three Empties limped through the farmland. Everyone in the vehicle was silent, and Gabriel could feel the others looking out into the field just as he was, and watching the three creatures walk aimlessly through it.

Gabriel re-focused his attention on the road and could feel the boy looking up to him. Dylan was awaiting a response. Finally, one came, but not from Gabriel.

"Buddy, we don't know why they're here," Marcus said. "But we're going to make sure that they don't hurt you, okay?"

Dylan looked back at Marcus, and then stared over at Gabriel as he navigated the vehicle around a small group of Empties and an abandoned semi-truck that was taking up a large portion of the highway.

"Do you think... God sent them?"

Gabriel glanced into the rearview mirror to see if anyone else looked as if they'd respond. When no one did, he broke the awkward silence.

"Why would God send something to kill us?"

Dylan shrugged. "Maybe he's mad at us."

Gabriel was a man of no faith. He grew up in a Catholic home, but quit going to church after going off to college and living on his own. He simply didn't believe in all the things the Bible had to say about rights and wrongs, life and death. But, he wasn't sure of the boy's beliefs and allegiances, so he decided to take the high road.

"Dylan, I don't think that a loving God would send anything down here to hurt us. I mean..."

"Look out!" The yell came from Holly in the very rear of the truck.

Gabriel looked ahead and saw the SUV heading straight for a fire truck parked in the middle of the road.

He reacted quickly and turned the wheel hard to his left, the sound of screeching tires and the aroma of burning rubber moving through the autumn air. Behind him, everyone in the vehicle was in a panic, yelling out, and Gabriel struggled to regain control of the truck.

But he couldn't.

The SUV swerved off of the road, flying over a ditch and rolled into the grass just on the other side.

With Gabriel's foot still on the brakes, the vehicle slid in the grass and stopped as it collided with a tree.

Steam rose from the engine and the air bags deployed.

Inside the truck, no one moved.

But outside, the Empties loitering on the highway were making their way toward the truck.

CHAPTER EIGHT

Jessica

Jessica had almost fallen back to sleep in the chair when the door to the room opened. She nearly hopped out of her skin and the nurse herself jumped in reaction to seeing how she'd frightened Jessica.

"Oh, I'm sorry!" Sarah said.

Jessica sat up straight in the chair, then sighed and rubbed the side of her head. She watched Sarah walk over to her bed and check the various machines connected to Melissa, recording data on a chart as she did.

"She doing about the same? No movement?" Sarah asked.

Jessica shook her head. "Not from what I've seen."

Sarah took a few notes, then looked back over to Jessica. "How about you? How's your shoulder?"

"Actually, much better today, thanks."

Sarah placed the clipboard back on the table beside the bed, then asked, "You up for a little walk?"

Jessica looked over to Melissa, seeing the woman in the same state she'd been in since they arrived. While she wanted to be here when Melissa awoke, she knew that it would be a futile task, simply *waiting*. So, she looked up to the smiling nurse and nodded.

"Sure."

***

Sarah led Jessica down the hallway to a small room near the front corridor. She went inside and picked up a large plastic tote, then smiled at Jessica. “Laundry day.”

“Do you do everyone’s laundry?”

“It’s not a huge deal. It’s not like everyone has very much. I mainly just end up washing sheets and linens.”

Sarah rested the bin on the ground and then walked back into the room, returning moments later with an additional laundry basket in tow, which had wheels and a handle.

“Mind pulling this one?”

“Not at all.”

Jessica used the hand on her good arm to grab the bin, and they walked back down the hallway.

The two women went from one room to the next, collecting the dirty laundry from the floor. Sarah explained to Jessica that the survivors occupying the hospital had been instructed to just leave their dirty clothes or linens on the floor just inside the door, and whoever had laundry duty next would come by and pick it up.

Once they’d gathered all the dirty laundry, they headed back toward the front of the hospital wing, and Sarah led them to a door and opened it.

“Wash is through here.” The two women headed inside.

***

The small laundry room had been built inside one of the guest lounges for visitors to use if they were required to have an extended stay at the hospital. They’d begun to load the washing machine with the pile of laundry when Jessica finally turned and asked the question that had been on her mind.

"What happened here?"

Sarah stopped, mid-lean over a laundry bin, while collecting another pile of linens. She dropped them as she stood back up, looking at the wall for a moment before sitting down in the nearest plastic chair.

Jessica leaned back against the washing machine and ran her hand through her hair.

"I'm sorry to have asked," Jessica said.

Sarah looked down to the floor and shook her head. "No, it's okay. It's just still really... new, you know?"

The young nurse cleared her throat and then finally spoke, keeping her eyes focused on the ground.

"I was making my rounds, checking in on different patients. My shift had only started about a half hour before, so I was seeing some of them for the first time. I went into a room where a young boy was, maybe around twelve years old. His name was Harrison. He was recovering from surgery. The day before, his dog had run out into the street and he'd chased after it. The guy driving was allegedly text messaging when he hit the kid."

"Asshole," Jessica mumbled.

"Yeah, no shit," Sarah added. "Anyway, I'd gone in to check on him. His surgery had gone well and he was resting. There had been a good bit of internal bleeding, which is always scary, but the doctor had done a good job and stabilized the boy. When I walked in, he shot me a big smile, which is always satisfying to see when you know a child is in pain. Harrison's mother was in the room with him. We talked for a few moments, and then I went on with doing some of my normal procedural stuff.

"While I was checking his blood-pressure, I heard a thud on the ground behind me and Harrison cried out. When I turned around, his mother was on the ground. I kneeled down and checked her pulse and, of course, there wasn't one. Almost at the same time, I heard the panic in the hallway.

"I rushed out of the room and the entire hospital was in a panic. There were bodies on the floor, people leaned over performing CPR. Honestly, I didn't know what to do. There was so much going on, it was as if I had been dropped right in the middle of a war zone. I stopped and tried to help a few people, until I remembered that I'd left Harrison back in his room with his mother collapsed next to him. So, I hurried back to him."

Sarah began to cry, and Jessica reached over and put her hand on the young woman's shoulder. Sarah took her hand, and let the tears flow. After a few moments, she continued.

"She was... on top of him. The screams... they were like nothing I'd ever heard before. Blood sprayed from both sides of the bed, staining the mattress. I started to run to help the boy, but when his mother looked up at me, I stopped dead in my tracks. She was one of *them*, and I watched her tear her own son apart."

Sarah couldn't hold back now. Jessica watched the girl slump over and her shoulders begin to move up and down as she cried. She patted Sarah on her back, and knelt down to embrace her.

"It's okay. We don't have to talk about it anymore."

Sarah picked up her head and wiped her eyes. She shook her head.

"No, it's okay. I need to." She sniffled, and moved her

hand under her nose to wipe it down. Sarah took a deep breath, and then started again.

"She moved to where I could see the boy... at least, what was left of him. It was horrible. I've seen people come into the hospital after devastating car wrecks, but I'd never seen anything like this.

"Then, the boy's mother was crawling over the bed toward me. I thought of running for the door, but the screams outside were deafening. I could hear people running up and down the halls, yelling out, and could hear what I now know was the snarling of these monsters. My back was against the door to a bathroom, so I turned around and trapped myself inside. When I went to lock the door, I couldn't. The damn doors on these patient bathrooms don't have locks. Within seconds, she was banging at the door. I pulled on the handle, just waiting for her to try and turn it. But all she did was bang and slam on it instead of trying to open it. I couldn't stop crying and trembling. All I wanted was to be home in my bed."

Jessica was covering her mouth, just listening to the story. "How long did you stay in there?"

"It was at least a couple of hours before I heard the door to the room open. I heard gunfire coming from somewhere inside the hospital. I jumped and cried more with every burst I heard. Then, the door to the room opened, and the banging at the door finally stopped. A loud gunshot rang through the room, followed by a crash. The snarling stopped, and I fell back against the wall, crying and shaking. I couldn't feel my hand from gripping the door handle so tight.

"When the door to the bathroom did finally open, I

screamed and balled myself up, waiting for one of the creatures to attack me. Instead, I turned to see a hand extended and a familiar face."

"Lawrence?" Jessica asked.

Sarah nodded.

"When I walked out into the hallway, I couldn't believe my eyes. And the smell was awful. There were bodies everywhere. Lawrence led me to a room where the rest of the survivors were hiding. He came back a bit later with Trevor, who had been helping him clear the place out."

"What did you guys do with the bodies?" Jessica asked.

"We spent the rest of that afternoon moving them into a couple of the stairwells. It was exhausting, but we were at least able to get *some* of the smell out of here."

"What about the rest of the hospital?"

"Lawrence, Brandon, and this guy Kyle went down to the floor below us. Lawrence and Brandon barely made it back. Kyle... he didn't. Ever since then, we've kept ourselves isolated up here. Apparently, it was really bad, and Lawrence doesn't want to risk looking around, at least not yet. If enough of those things get up here, we're done."

Jessica just crouched there, letting everything Sarah told her sink in. She thought about the hotel, and what happened after her escape. Did anyone survive? Maybe there was a small group there, like there was here. Just maybe some of her friends from her old workplace were still alive. She wasn't sure if she'd ever know.

Sarah stood up and filled the washing machine with as many dirty clothes as she could before turning it on.

"Come on," Sarah said to Jessica. "Let's go grab some

food and check on your friend; then we can come back later and throw this stuff in the dryer."

CHAPTER NINE

Lawrence

"We've got to make a stop," Lawrence told David. They'd driven for about an hour, occasionally seeing survivors pass by in their own vehicles, but not finding anyone stranded. Lawrence would wave at the other vehicles in hopes that they would stop, but they didn't, and David kept reiterating how people had already lost their trust and hope in others.

Lawrence was getting a strange vibe from David. He couldn't exactly put his finger on it, but something about the way he'd been acting was just rubbing him the wrong way. He was about to ask David about how he ended up in a ditch on the side of the highway before Lawrence had rescued him when David spoke first.

"Where are we going?"

Lawrence thought of changing the subject, but they were close to their destination, and so he decided against it.

"There's a small clinic up the road here. It's a little off the beaten path, so it may not have been raided yet. I know some of the people that worked there so I want to go check it out."

He looked over to David, who didn't respond. The man just sat there, looking out the window.

"You know how to fire a gun?" Lawrence asked.

David looked over to him and nodded. "I can hold my own, yeah."

"Good."

With one hand on the wheel, Lawrence reached down and grabbed a pistol that was hidden between the driver's side door and his seat. He held it in his hand where David could see it, all while staring at the man. He was trying to get a read on the mysterious man to see if he should give him the gun or not. In the end, he knew that it wouldn't be safe for him to go into the clinic alone, and he couldn't send David in unarmed. So, he handed David Ellis the small firearm.

David accepted the weapon into his hand as Lawrence put all his focus back onto the road. He heard David pop out the clip to confirm that the gun was loaded.

"It's a 0.38. Should give you plenty of punch to take any of those things down."

"Thanks," David said.

Lawrence looked up the road and saw the exit he needed to take to get to the clinic.

"Here we go," Lawrence said.

As Lawrence continued to drive toward the exit, he heard a window open. He looked over and saw David pointing the gun outside with both hands gripping the weapon. Up the road just a bit, Lawrence saw one of the creatures limping down the shoulder on the other side of the metal railing. David had the gun focused on it.

As they passed by the beast, Lawrence heard David fire off a round, and then he looked into the passenger side mirror.

Lawrence could just see the beast roll down the hill and come to a stop at the bottom, lying motionless.

He looked over to David, who was rolling up the window

with the gun in his lap. The man never looked over toward Lawrence. He only continued to stare outside, and Lawrence wondered what the man could have been thinking.

***

David

"It's just up ahead," Lawrence said.

Just as Lawrence had told him earlier, the small clinic sat off an uninhabited road. They must have been on the outskirts of Knoxville, because there wasn't much out here. As they got closer, David noticed something. Behind the building was a large wooden structure with chain link fence built into the sides of it. It ran a good twenty yards off the back of the building. Then, David could finally read the sign out front: Volunteer Kennels.

Lawrence pulled into the parking lot, and David watched as four Empties banged at the front door of the building. As the ambulance approached, the creatures turned around and walked toward them.

"Alright, let's..."

But before Lawrence could finish, David was already out of the vehicle.

He walked toward the first Empty, raised the handgun, and fired a bullet right through its skull. Then, he hit the creature walking next to it. The next Empty was a few yards away and, still moving forward, he fired without missing that one, too. With one remaining, David stopped. He waited for the beast to get within just a few feet of him and, as it reached out to grab him, he kicked it in the stomach as hard as he could. The Empty stumbled to the ground, and David looked down at it. Just as it was about to reach for him, he lifted his leg and slammed his size eleven boot down onto the thing's skull, crushing it.

David stood there, looking down at the last Empty. Barking from the dogs inside the kennels sang through the air. The way his boot had sandwiched the thing's brain into the concrete tickled him funny on the inside. It made him feel good to end a being and to watch it stop moving. He only wished the Empties had the obligation to breathe so he could have watched the thing draw its last breath.

From behind him, David heard a door shut from the ambulance and he turned around to see Lawrence looking toward him with his jaw dropped.

"You're crazy, man!" Lawrence exclaimed.

David turned his body to face the shocked black man. "I'll need more ammo and a knife, if you've got one." He walked toward Lawrence, who was still just standing there in awe of what he'd just witnessed.

Lawrence walked to the back of the ambulance and, when he came back, he had a backpack on and he offered David a bowie knife. It rested in a sheath, and David secured the holster for the blade around his waist. David slipped the extra clip into his pocket, turned around, and headed for the front door.

***

"Cover me," David told Lawrence, who was standing right behind him.

David used one hand to slowly open the door. The dogs were barking so loudly that, if there was an Empty on the other side of this door snarling at him, he was apt not to even hear it, but his gun was drawn just in case.

The door creaked open with no trouble.

Once the door was open all the way, the smell hit him immediately. David brought his free hand up to cover his nose, and turned around to see Lawrence doing the same.

"What the fuck is that?" Lawrence asked. The man was a paramedic, and would have been inured to just about any foul smell by now, one would think. But this was awful.

David entered the clinic and saw the scattered remains of what had once been a human plastered all over the tile floor. It was chewed up, with blood and pieces of tissue, guts, and organs spread across the floor and wall, and David put himself on high alert. There were Empties here.

He turned around and held his pistol up in front of his face, ready to take down any creatures that came across his path. David watched Lawrence pass through the door and look down at the body. He covered his mouth and his eyes widened.

"Keep a lookout," David said. "There's got to be some of them in here."

Lawrence nodded in acknowledgement, then turned around and raised his own gun.

In front of them was a welcome counter. Behind it, there was a door that presumably led to offices and an operating room, while beside the counter, there were two double doors with a sign on one of them that read "Kennels - Employees Only". The barking was coming from beyond those doors.

Lawrence looked to David. "I'm going to go check this door behind the counter. Why don't you go check through those doors and see if you find anything back there?"

David nodded and approached the double doors as

Lawrence walked behind the counter through a small swinging gate.

The double doors had two square windows, and the barking grew louder as David approached them. When he got to where he could see through the windows, he saw *them*.

Three Empties stood along a narrow hallway. Lined down one side was chain link fence with individual gates every few feet. The Empties were standing in front of them, banging and pulling on the metal fencing, trying to bust through the fence to get to the barking meat inside.

David checked to make sure the gun was loaded, and then hesitated. He had a feeling building inside him... a need. He slipped the gun into the band of his pants, then reached for the knife. Pulling it from the sheath, he examined the blade up and down. It was fairly clean, free of blood, and begging for him to christen it.

David wet his lips, circling them with his tongue. He then smiled, grasped the knife with a solemn grip, and pushed through the doors.

***

Lawrence

The horrific odor along with the ongoing barking was giving Lawrence a splitting headache. The smell was a disgusting combination of death and dog shit, and Lawrence wondered if he would ever be able to wash the stench off of himself. He could hardly focus his attention on his surroundings as his temples pounded. The dogs barking in the kennels a on the other side of the wall didn't help either. All he wanted was to see if any survivors were here, get what he needed, and get out of this place.

He walked all the way through a short hall with doors on either side to a large operating room. He slowly lowered the gun once he was certain the room was clear. No one was around.

The idea that they were going to find any survivors was becoming futile. Since there wasn't anyone around, Lawrence shifted his focus on trying to find supplies they could use at the hospital. There were a few specific items they needed, and he decided to fill the remaining space in his backpack with anything else they could use at the hospital. The main item on his mental checklist was anesthetics. The wing of the hospital they were trapped in did not have a heavy supply, and he wanted to make sure that he had some in case he'd have to try to perform any emergency procedures that would require a sedative. There was a room connected to the operation room, and he walked through the door hoping to find the vet clinic's supply of drugs.

"Bingo!" he said.

Lawrence pulled off his backpack and started grabbing anything that appeared useful, including the local anesthetic Lidocaine.

Once he'd filled his bag, he turned to head out of the room.

He went back through to the operating room and immediately dropped his bag as a creature reached out to him. It had already gripped his shoulders before he could reach for the gun on his hip.

Lawrence gasped as the thing spit into his face, chomping its teeth. It pushed him back against the wall, and Lawrence's grip on the gun almost slipped.

"Help!" he yelled out. "David!" His scream was blocked out by the snarling monster and the dogs barking in the distance.

The creature had once been an overweight man, heavier than Lawrence by at least fifty pounds, and its strength was evident. Lawrence couldn't unpin himself from the wall.

It was just inches from Lawrence's face now, clicking its jaw repeatedly right over his nose.

In a last-ditch effort, Lawrence mustered every bit of strength he had left in him and shoved the creature. It worked, but the thing still kept a hold of him and they both went stumbling over a table in the middle of the floor.

Lawrence landed on his back and arched, feeling the pain shoot down his spine. He looked over to see the beast trying to roll over toward him, and Lawrence reached for his gun. It wasn't there.

He sat up and saw that it had fallen out and was on the ground about ten feet away.

As he started to get up and go for the pistol, the thing grabbed his arm, holding him back. Lawrence screamed as its nails dug into his forearm. He fell down, and the creature was trying to pull him toward it. Lawrence tried to beat it off of him, but the beast wouldn't let go. The thing caught one of the punches, but Lawrence was able to pull his hand away just as the thing was about to bite into him.

He looked away from the creature, trying to find something, anything, that could help him.

Just within his reach was a scalpel that must have fallen off of the table when they toppled over it. As he went to reach for it, the thing made a lunge at him, and Lawrence had to turn quickly and push it away. He ended up rolling on top of the creature, pushing down on its arms as it tried to bite his exposed wrists.

Lawrence looked over at the small scalpel, biting his lip. He decided to make a jump at it.

He let go of the beast and dove toward the scalpel.

He accidentally grabbed it by the blade and cut his hand, then dropped the scalpel back onto the floor. The mistake gave the creature time to grab him again, but as the thing tried to pull him toward itself, Lawrence was able to get another hold on the scalpel.

Lawrence took a deep breath, rolled over, and drove the small blade into the thing's eye.

Within moments, the grip on him loosened, and he rolled onto his back.

Staring at the ceiling, Lawrence spread his arms out like an angel, and lay there, breathing heavily as the beast ceased moving for good.

***

David

David stood in the middle of the hallway in silence.

Blood was everywhere. It coated the walls, covered the floor, and stained his clothes. He looked over and even saw crimson on the coat of one of the white dogs. It was barking at him, but he managed to block out every noise in the room, so all he saw was its jaw snapping. The bodies of the three Empties lay motionless nearby, and he stood over the final one he'd slain, the bloody knife still in his grasp. Mentally, he traveled to another place.

As David walked toward the door, he saw something he

hadn't noticed before. There was a fourth carcass on the ground, much smaller than that of a human. Though there was hardly anything left, he could tell from the fur around the blood and entrails that it was the remains of a dog.

He cocked his head, and smiled slightly at the sight of more death.

David stepped over the animal, and the other two Empties, and walked back through the double doors.

***

When he walked behind the front counter and entered the back room, the double doors to the O.R. were already open. David could see Lawrence sitting on the ground next to a large table with his back to him. He wasn't moving, just sitting there with his shoulders steadily rising and falling.

This is it.

The man wasn't fit to lead the group. David knew it. He could see so much potential in the hospital and the group that was there. David saw no reason to expand their group. They could survive with those they already had. Lawrence had other plans, and David could end those ideas right now.

David sheathed the knife and pulled the handgun from his waist.

Carefully, he crept closer to Lawrence. David was a damned good shot, and knew he wouldn't have to get very close to blow the back of the man's head out.

He'd tasted the ceasing of the Empties moments earlier, and now he was ready to feed off the ending of a real life. The feeling, the desire, and the craving were inside him. He just had to fulfill them.

The incessant barking of the dogs blocked out the sounds

of his footsteps as well as the sound of him cocking the gun as he reached the door to the large room.

David raised the pistol and aimed.

A noise distracted him, and David turned just as an Empty rushed out from a door and came at him.

It was just about his size, wearing a white overcoat. The Empty had David around his neck, driving him against the wall while David clutched at its arms and tried to push back against his chest.

A loud bang rang into David's left ear, and the weight of the Empty left him as it fell to the ground.

David looked over and saw Lawrence standing just five feet away from him, holding the gun up to the head level of where the Empty had stood. Like David, Lawrence had blood all over his clothes.

Gasping, the black man looked at David. He reached into his pocket, and tossed David a set of keys, which he caught in his free hand.

"Get me the fuck outta here," Lawrence gasped. "You're driving."

CHAPTER TEN

Will

When Will opened his eyes again, he was lying on his stomach in a daze. He wasn't sure how much time had passed, and he could hardly remember where he was. His ears rang, and though he heard a distorted collection of noises around him, he couldn't identify any of them. After a few moments, his vision, though blurry, began to return. His hands were resting on the carpeted interior lining the SUV's cargo area floor, and he could feel the weight of something resting on the back of his legs.

Will tried to push himself up but quickly fell back down. He felt his blood rush to his head, and put his hand near his temple and rubbed the area where it hurt the most. When he looked at his hand moments later, there was blood on it.

Again, he tried to get up, but the weight on top of him made it difficult. He simultaneously lifted his legs and slid to the left, and felt the weight slowly let off of him. He looked down and noticed that Holly had been on top of him. Her eyes were closed, and she had a large blood stain on her own head.

"Oh, shit, Holly!"

He grabbed her by the shoulders and gently shook her, but she wouldn't come to. Will grabbed her arm and checked her wrist for a pulse. Though faint, it did exist.

In an instant, Will's hearing became clear and he heard the Empties banging on the truck from all sides, and the frantic yelling from within the SUV.

He fell down and covered his ears once he heard the first gunshot. He stayed there for a moment, curled up with his ears covered. The gunshots continued from within the truck, with frantic yelling surrounding them.

Will sat up again and saw Marcus firing out of the broken back seat window on the driver's side. He looked toward the front of the truck and saw that they had hit a tree. Gabriel was still in the driver's seat, his head buried into an air bag, and Will wasn't sure if he was alive. Dylan was in the front seat, covering his ears and screaming. Marcus was in front of Will, and Miranda was...

Where is Miranda?

When he looked out the driver's side of the SUV, he noticed a small group of Empties gathered around something. For a brief second, he saw one of the things pull its head up and spit something pink into the air while chomping its jaws.

"I need you, man!" Marcus yelled. "We're fuckin' surrounded. Miranda's dead, man. They fuckin' got her. And I'm not sure if Gabriel is alive or not. But, I need you!" The weapons were stored behind the front seats in the floor, giving Marcus easy access to them. He reached down and grabbed a rifle and a Glock, then handed them to Will.

Will felt a pit in his stomach as he came to realize that the horde was ripping Miranda apart. He wanted to throw up, but stopped himself.

"Will! Focus!"

Will rapidly blinked his eyes a few times and shook his head, then started to assess their situation. Most of the Empties on the driver's side of the vehicle were distracted by the feasting on Miranda's body. The group on the passenger side and the back of the truck—right on the other side of the glass from where Will sat—were banging on the truck and rocking it back and forth, making it even more difficult for Will to focus.

"I need you to give me some cover!" Marcus said.

Will slanted his eyes. "Cover? For what?"

"We can't stay here. I've got to go and get us another vehicle."

Will shook his head. "Nah, man. You're still beat to shit. I'll go."

"Look who's talkin'. You should see your face, brotha."

"Seriously, Marcus. Let me go."

One of the creatures reached through the open window where Miranda once sat, and Marcus put a bullet between its eyes immediately. The beast hung motionless over the window, halfway inside the vehicle.

Marcus sighed in relief and shook his head at Will. "Alright. What are you going to do?"

Will looked out and saw several vehicles near the fire engine they'd almost collided with. From what he could see, it appeared that the only Empties on that side of the SUV were the ones banging on it, trying to get inside.

"I've gotta make a run for one of those cars," Will said.

"You know how to hot-wire it?" Marcus asked.

Will nodded. "Yeah, I think so."

"I hope so."

"I'm gonna have to go out that door you're leaning against," Will told Marcus. "It's the only way. Here." Will handed the rifle back to Marcus. "I need to travel light. I'll just take the .45. Leave that dead Empty in the window. It should fill up enough space to keep any others from reaching in." Will looked up to the front seat. "Dylan."

The boy was crying with his hands over his ears and didn't look up.

"Dylan!" Will yelled.

The boy looked up, and Will looked into his bloodshot eyes.

"Buddy, I know you're scared, but we need your help, okay?"

The boy nodded.

"You need to watch Marcus' back and let him know if any danger is coming from behind him. Can you do that?"

Dylan nodded again, then sat up straight in his seat, moving his hair from in front of his eyes, though still crying.

"Good."

Will looked down at Holly and ran his fingers through her hair. He could feel a lump right where he figured their heads had collided during the turbulence of the crash. He leaned down and kissed her on the cheek. "I'll be back," he whispered. He then hopped over the seat and sat next to Marcus. They switched places so that Will could be next to the door. There were two Empties right on the other side of it.

Will took a deep breath. "Alright. On the count of three, I'm gonna break open the window so we can clear a path before I open the door and run for it. You ready?"

"Ready!" Marcus said.

"One... two..."

Will took a deep breath and mumbled to himself, "Please, be with me."

Then, at the count of "One!" Will shattered the window with the butt of the rifle and fired consecutive shots into each of the two Empties' skulls, then opened the door and jumped out.

A creature came at him from behind the truck, and he saved a bullet by pulling the knife off his waist and driving it into the thing's skull. He then looked back and saw that a couple of the Empties were pulling away from Miranda's body and moving toward him.

"Go!" Marcus yelled.

Will watched Marcus turn to shoot the Empties leaving the body, but they were already behind the truck and out of the view of any open window. Will knew that Marcus couldn't break the rear window with Holly lying unconscious in the back. It'd be too easy for one of the things to reach in and hurt her.

"Fucking go!" Marcus yelled again. "Or I'm gonna shoot your ass and run to one of those cars myself!"

Finally, Will came out of his trance and hurried away from the truck.

He had to dodge the remains of the dead in the middle of the road, and a couple of vultures flew away from the rotting corpses when he began to run.

There were an array of abandoned vehicles to choose from, but Will just ran to the first one he could get to. When he tried to open the door, it was locked, and an Empty appeared in the window and banged on the glass. Will fell backward, landing on his tailbone, grimacing. He then heard a snarl, and one of the creatures was over him. He quickly drew his Glock and unloaded a round into the Empty's head, rolling out of the way before it fell on him.

He jumped to his feet and ran to the next car he could reach. Behind him, he heard gunshots and bodies hitting the pavement. He took a quick glance back and saw Marcus firing at the Empties out of the window. It looked like the entire group was migrating away from Miranda's body now.

Will readied his firearm and pulled the handle on the door to a four-door sedan. It opened, and he prepared to shoot if one of the creatures jumped out at him, but none did. He slid into the driver's seat and looked for keys. He checked in all the obvious places—under the sun visor, in the glove box, in the sunglasses compartment—but he couldn't find any. He got out of the seat and squatted down next to the car, and opened the compartment under the steering wheel, exposing the wiring.

As he started to mess with the wires, he heard a continuous snarl amidst a fury of gunshots.

"Will! Look out!" Marcus shouted.

Will stood, and an Empty was in his face, pushing on the door and pinning him between the door and the body of the vehicle. It was dressed in a fireman's uniform, wearing a helmet with a shield covering its face. It leaned in to Will's face, and if it hadn't been for the shield the thing was wearing, it would have easily been able to bite Will.

Will pushed the door, sending the Empty stumbling back, but it stayed on its feet. He pulled up his gun and fired, but the bullet ricocheted off of the helmet, and the creature kept walking toward him. After another two shots, the gun clicked; it had run out of ammo.

"Shit!"

He went to reach for the knife, but the beast was already on him.

It pushed Will back against the car. He could just see over the thing's shoulder, where Marcus was unloading more rounds into Empties who were trying to come over to Will. He gripped the creature's jacket, which was slick with blood, making it difficult to keep a good grasp on it.

The Empty was a few inches taller than Will, giving it leverage. Its face was right over the top of Will's, and saliva was dripping off of the bottom of the shield and down onto Will's cheek.

Will let out a grunt, and pushed the creature back. It had a hold on him still and they both tumbled to the ground.

When they hit the highway, the thing's helmet flew off, freeing its jaws. It snapped at Will's right hand, which was still gripping the jacket at the shoulder, and Will quickly moved his hand before it bit him.

As Will went to put his hand back to hold it down, the Empty shot up and came at his arm.

Right as it was about to bite Will's forearm, a single gunshot rang through the air and blood sprayed onto Will's face. The Empty fell limp and let go.

Will wiped his face and looked up.

Marcus was standing halfway between the truck and him, slowly lowering the rifle.

Will stood up and narrowed his eyes at Marcus.

"You could have fuckin' shot me!"

Marcus tilted his head and smiled with a single, muffled laugh. "Yeah, you're welcome."

Will patted down his shirt and his pants, shaking his head.

"Let's just see if we can get one of these things started and move Holly and Gabriel into it, okay?" Marcus asked.

Marcus walked over to the sedan that Will was trying to jump when the former firefighter attacked him. Will watched him kneel down and begin to play with the wires.

At Will's feet, the Empty lay motionless. He looked at it, wondering how many times the man in the suit had escaped a life-threatening situation when he'd been alive, only to have it end like this.

Will kneeled down and looked the thing in the eyes. They were still open, a pale white. He scanned its body, until he noticed something hanging out of the right pocket of its pants.

He reached in and grabbed the object, smiling.

"Hey!" Will said to Marcus.

Marcus turned back and Will dangled the keys in the air.

"I think I got us a ride."

CHAPTER ELEVEN

Lawrence

Trevor and Sam were waiting to let them in when Lawrence and David returned. As the ambulance pulled through the makeshift gate, Lawrence heard three gunshots muting the two snarling beasts that were standing near the gate as David pulled up to it.

Lawrence stepped out of the ambulance and the two men immediately rushed over.

"Holy shit!" Trevor said. "You guys alright?"

Lawrence nodded. "Fine. Just a close call."

He had an intense pain in his right shoulder. Fighting with the large beast and trying to hold it off of him had fatigued his muscles, and his brain was just now starting to receive the signal, the adrenaline finally wearing off. Blood stained his clothes and his hands.

If Lawrence looked like he had been to hell, David looked like he was the fucking president of the underworld. Blood was everywhere, barely leaving a clean place on his clothes or his body.

Sam and Trevor stood next to Lawrence as the three men watched David step out of the vehicle and head inside without saying anything. He had on a short-sleeved shirt and his arms were covered in red. When he walked, he did so with a slow limp.

"What the fuck happened to you?" Sam asked David, but the man didn't turn around. Lawrence, Sam, and Trevor watched as David entered the hospital.

Behind him in the distance, Lawrence heard snarls growing louder as they came up the ramp of the parking garage toward the gate. He took a deep breath and took a step toward the door.

Sam put his hand on Lawrence's shoulder and asked, "What happened?"

Lawrence sighed and found a clean place on the back of his hand that he could use to rub his eyes. He then held up the bag he had in his hand and said, "We got some supplies." He threw the bag over his shoulder, grimacing as the sudden movement shot a pain into the joint that connected his arm to it.

"Here," Trevor said, extending his hand out and offering to take the bag.

Lawrence glared at him for a moment and then sighed. He removed the bag from his shoulder and handed it over to Trevor.

"Thanks," Lawrence said.

"No problem."

Lawrence nodded toward the door. "Come on. Let's go inside and I'll fill you guys in on what happened."

***

David

David reached his room free and clear of anyone seeing him. He wouldn't have stopped to talk to anyone if they'd tried, thus avoiding the inevitable awkwardness that would have arisen. David only wanted to get to his room and be alone.

Once inside, he shut the door behind him. He looked around the room for something heavy enough to put against the door so that no one from the outside could open it, but nothing would suffice. The closest thing was the bed, but even if he put the wheels in the lock position, it was still probably too lightweight to prevent anyone from getting inside.

He walked to the bathroom to take a piss, and then washed his hands and arms. The darkened, dried blood filled the sink. He watched the white porcelain turn deep crimson as he scrubbed vigorously. David looked into the mirror and splashed water onto his face. The man looking back at him was a stranger. Just days ago, he'd been a successful business owner; a millionaire and an eligible bachelor. Now, he was nothing more than another person trying to survive in this new world. His money didn't mean shit anymore as far as he could tell.

David looked a little further down in the mirror and tended to a cut on his left pectoral. During his struggle with the last Empty, the creature had scratched him really good. He grabbed a towel and applied pressure to the scratch to try and cease the light bleeding.

His eyes moved to other scars on his body.

In various places on his chest and his stomach, David had permanent cuts and scratches. He avoided looking at them as much as possible, desperately wanting to forget the memories trapped inside the wounds.

But, deep down, he knew that to forget the origins of his wounds would only weaken him.

***

October, 1984
Texas

He remembered every detail about the last time it happened.

The boy was sitting in the closet under the stairs, where he and his brother would often go to hide. The closet was only used to store coats and a couple of boxes full of junk, so there was plenty of room for the two boys to fit inside.

This particular night, James Robert Ellis had finally gone too far.

David sat in the small closet alone, while in the other room, his mother begged for James to stop. It wasn't as if young David hadn't heard it before. During his thirteen years of life, the boy couldn't remember a time when his father hadn't beaten his mother. Recently, though, the beatings had gotten worse. And they weren't just limited to David's mother. His father had beaten him and his little brother, Michael, as well. Michael was two years younger than David and was upstairs in his bedroom. David could only hope at the time that his younger brother was asleep like he was supposed to be, and like David, should have been.

"Robert, please!" David's mother cried.

David heard the glass bottle slam onto the table, and could distinctly hear the heavy breathing of his father as he grunted, then connected with another blow, the slap obvious through the stale air.

While his mother sobbed uncontrollably, David didn't cry. He had long passed the point of becoming immune to the beatings. David knew he would be next. It hurt him to know that his mother was in pain, but he wanted to keep a straight face for when his father came after him. He didn't want to give the son of a bitch the luxury of seeing him cry while the man, enraged in a drunken state, beat his oldest son with the same black, leather belt that he'd used many times over.

"What?" David's father yelled.

David could hear his mother crying more loudly now. He heard his father growl, and his mother let out a deafening scream. David came off the wall he was leaning against and sat up straight. There was a bang, followed by glass shattering, and then a loud thud.

He jumped to his feet and ran out of the closet toward the kitchen.

When David reached the dining room, his father was already waiting for him. He looked down and saw his mother lying facedown on the linoleum floor. Blood was coming out of her forehead. He wanted to run to her, but feared that his dad might harm him even more than he was already going to if he tried to help her.

"You son of a bitch," David mumbled.

His father took a swig out of the whiskey bottle, wiped his mouth with the back of his hand, and glared down at his oldest son.

"Boy, I'll teach you to talk to me like that!"

And for the next twenty minutes, that's exactly what his father did.

***

Just over a week later, David was heading out the door to

go hunting with his younger brother and a slightly more sober version of his father. He watched as his mother planted a kiss onto his stoic father's cheek before leaning down to give him one.

"Love you, son."

"Love you, too, Mom."

She kissed Michael, told him the same, and the two boys joined their father in his pickup truck.

***

The only sound in the truck was that of outlaw country music coming from the stereo. None of them spoke on the way to the land where they were going to hunt. It belonged to a friend of David's father, a man who James had worked with at the factory for almost nine years. The man had supposedly inherited the land when his own father had died, and allowed some of his friends, including James Ellis, to come hunt on the land during deer season.

David sat in the middle of the bench seat between his father and his little brother. He glanced over at Michael, whose eye had swollen overnight from the beating their father had given him. David looked up at his father, who didn't acknowledge him. He focused on the road, smacking the snuff between his gums, and mouthing the words to Waylon on the radio.

The truck turned down the bumpy dirt road that led to the hunting area; David and his brother bounced up and down on the old seats.

"You boys better keep God damned quiet when we're out there, you hear me? I don't want you scarin' no deer away," their father said.

"Yes, father," Michael replied.

David didn't say anything.

Out of the corner of his eye, he could see his father glance down at him a couple of times.

"You hear me, boy?"

David narrowed his eyes and continued to face forward.

"Ouch!" David cried out as his father drove his right elbow into his arm.

"You better not ignore me, boy, or I'll make both your eyes look like your brother's."

David rubbed his arm and took a deep breath. "Yes, sir."

At the end of the dirt road, the truck came to a stop, and David's father stepped out of the driver's seat.

"Come'on boys."

The two children climbed out of the truck and followed their father.

***

David stood behind a bush, eyeing a deer that was grazing twenty yards away. He licked his lips in anticipation of firing a shot. When they hunted, they sometimes stayed together, while other times they'd separate. Today, their father had decided to split them all up. The boys had spent enough time hunting in the woods to be on their own. David assumed that his father wasn't exactly in the mood for quality time with his two boys, and that was fine with him. If their mother hadn't begged him to take them, James more than likely would have just gone alone.

As David sat there watching the animal and waiting for the right time to take a shot, he looked around at the vast open woods around him. *What if I just found Michael and we ran away? Just fled through these woods and never saw that asshole again?* The thought was intriguing. David hated his father, and the thought of independence from the bastard crawled up inside him.

There was a rustle in the leaves behind David, and the deer raised its head. The boy came out of his daydream of leaving his abusive father behind and hurried to aim, but it was too late.

The deer looked his way before running away into the trees.

David sighed and shook his head.

"Good job, faggot." The voice was that of his father.

David turned around to see the man walking toward him. He was about fifteen yards away, taking a swig straight out of a bottle of Jack Daniel's. He'd left his gun resting on a large rock just behind him. James stumbled over the sticks and leaves on the ground, and David thought the man could fall to the ground at any time.

"You just don't have it in ya to get the job done, do ya, boy?"

The anger crept up inside of David again. He glared right into his father's eyes. A sensation built up from the pit of his stomach. When he looked into his father's gaze, which was so much like his own, he saw nothing but emptiness. Hatred. David's palms were sweaty, and his arms were trembling.

"You're a fuckin' puss-ass loser, son. A no-good piece of shit!"

Right as the last word came out of his father's mouth, David raised the rifle up and aimed it directly at his hatred.

James raised his hands into the air. "What? You gonna

shoot me, son?" The man laughed.

His father stood within ten yards of David, and the boy had the gun pointed right at his chest, looking down the barrel with one open eye.

His father smiled from ear to ear. "You don't have the balls to pull that trigger, you little queer. Just wait until you put it down. I'm gonna beat the shit out of your brother in front of you, then I'm gonna beat the shit out of you. And your mother? I'll beat her ass just for making me drag you little faggots out here with me."

The feeling in David's stomach grew stronger. His heart was beating a hundred miles per hour, like it would erupt right out of his chest at any moment. His hands still trembled, and the gun made a faint clicking sound as he shook it.

David's father laughed again. "You're worthless."

He brought down the hand that held the bottle and took another long swig of the whiskey. Once the bottle had begun to tip back, James' eyes went wide and he reared the bottle back, preparing to throw it at his son.

Before he could, David pulled the trigger.

The glass bottle shattered on a rock next to James' feet. David watched his father look down at the blood seeping out of his chest, in complete shock at what had happened. The blast hit him in the left part of his chest. Blood poured out of the wound, turning the man's hands crimson as he clutched it.

James fell to his knees, gave one last look at his young son, and then fell onto his face.

David stood alone in the middle of the woods, staring at

the motionless body of his father. He felt no regret. No remorse. The man who'd brought him, his brother, and his beautiful mother so much pain was dead.

And David Ellis was changed forever.

CHAPTER TWELVE

Will

Since they'd been together, the fire truck was quite possibly the best thing that had happened to them. The large fire engine easily plowed over the Empties causing little to no damage to the vehicle. Marcus even collided with a few cars and they barely felt the impact. Will let Marcus drive since he claimed he had experience operating heavier machinery in the past. Will was thankful that Marcus felt well enough to drive now.

Dylan was asleep, sitting upright in one of the seats behind them. The two men laughed when the boy began to snore. Holly and Gabriel were lying on the floor of the truck in the back, still passed out from the crash. They were breathing and in stable condition, but Will and Marcus only hoped that they could find help soon.

Will was elated when he saw the large green sign reading: Knoxville 26. They were finally getting close.

"About damned time!" Marcus said.

Will leaned over and put his head into his hands. He looked up and Marcus was looking over at him.

"What's wrong, bro?" Marcus asked.

"I just hope we aren't too late, and I hope we can find them."

"We will, man. We will."

"It's taken too long, Marcus. What if they're hurt... or worse?"

"You can't think like that. You have to *believe* that we are going to find your mom and dad, and we will."

Will looked out the window and watched a group of Empties on the eastbound side of the interstate.

"I hope you're right."

***

Jessica

Jessica had finished up helping out with laundry and was now in the nurses' lounge making herself a sandwich. No one else was in there, which surprised her since it was around lunchtime.

Just as she finished making a peanut butter and jelly sandwich, the mysterious man she saw sitting alone in his room earlier walked in. She noticed his arms were stained with blood, though he smelled and otherwise appeared as though he had just showered. When he entered the room, he didn't even acknowledge her. He walked right past her to the refrigerator.

As he opened it, Jessica awkwardly cleared her throat.

"Uh, hi," she said.

The man turned around, holding a pitcher of sweet tea in his hand, and nodded at Jessica.

"I'm Jessica."

"David," the man said, pouring himself a glass.

"What happened to your arms?"

David looked down to the blood that was still painted on his forearms. "Got into a scuffle with a couple of Empties."

"A couple of what?"

"Nothing."

Jessica thought about asking the man why they called them that where he came from, but she was more interested in just that: where he came from.

"Why are you here? Where were you before?"

"Look, no offense, but I'm not really in the mood to talk."

"Oh, come on. What else are you gonna do?"

David sighed. "Nashville. I got out because there was nothing left there for me. Got stranded out on the highway. Lawrence picked me up."

"He's been great," Jessica said, speaking of Lawrence.

"Yeah, he's alright."

Jessica turned as she heard a door open and saw Sarah poke her head into the kitchen, panting.

"Jessica, come on. She's awake."

Without saying goodbye to David, Jessica ran out of the kitchen and headed for Melissa's room.

***

Gabriel

Katie Alexander was wearing his favorite outfit. He loved the way the jeans hugged his wife's hips and the simple white tank top she wore when the weather was warm. Sarah, his daughter, was at the park with them, running around and chasing after butterflies, trying to get one to land on her arm. He looked over and saw his wife's warm smile. He walked over to her and kissed her on the cheek, embracing her tightly. Her warm body rubbed up against his as her hand ran up his back and clutched his neck. He moved his head back and looked her in the eyes, leaning in and kissing her soft lips.

As he pulled away, he looked over toward his daughter again.

She was gone.

He ran around the park searching for Sarah, but he couldn't find her anywhere.

When he finally found her, the little girl's back was turned to him. She was staring at a tree where somebody had carved a broken heart.

"Sarah?" he said.

When the girl turned around, he cried out.

Sarah was Empty. Her eyes and skin had both turned pale, and her innocent voice had turned into a malicious snarl. As she approached him, his eyes went wide and he shook his head. Was this *really* his daughter?

He took a few steps back until he ran into something, and he turned around to see that his wife had also turned. Katie came at him, her mouth wide open, with saliva spilling from it, and she bit into his neck.

A moment later, he felt a sting on his leg and was running his fingers through his daughter's hair as she bit into his calf.

Then, it was as if he was watching a movie. He saw himself being savagely torn apart by the two people he loved most in the world. The green grass browned, and the sun quickly fell until everything was black.

The only thing Gabriel could hear was his own screaming.

***

When Gabriel awoke, he was panting. He rubbed his face, and the back of his hand came up moist with sweat.

He looked around, completely disoriented. The ride was bumpy, and he was lying on a hard surface. Next to him,

Holly was curled up with her eyes closed, and she sighed with each heavy breath. When he tried to sit up, he felt a rush to his head and quickly had to lie back down.

"Just stay down, bro," Will said. He was kneeling over Gabriel and placed a hand on his shoulder, encouraging Gabriel to follow his instructions. Dylan was also nearby, buckled into a seat and looking down at him.

"Where are we?" Gabriel asked, a haziness in his voice.

"A firetruck."

Gabriel narrowed his eyes. "What?"

"I'll explain when you're feeling a bit better."

"What happened?"

"We were in a car accident. You don't remember?"

Gabriel nodded. "Just barely. I remember swerving then running off the road. Everything went black after that. Did anyone get hurt?"

Will put his hand on his forehead and was silent.

"What, Will?"

"Miranda," Will said, removing his hand from his head and looking down into Gabriel's eyes.

Gabriel covered his eyes and shook his head. "Shit."

"She didn't die in the accident. The window by her busted out and I think she was hanging out of it. A group of Empties got her."

"Fuck."

Gabriel could feel the guilt creep up into him. He was driving when the accident happened. How could he ever live that down? Essentially, he killed a woman; a friend. He could never go back and fix that. As long as he lasted in this new world, he'd think about that every single day.

And what about the dream? What did it mean? While it might have meant nothing and only been a nightmare, Gabriel couldn't stop worrying that his wife and daughter had either turned into some of the walking creatures outside, or they'd been killed by them. The last few days had been the most difficult in his entire life. He felt absolutely hopeless, having not spoken to them. And while he knew that his best chance of staying alive was to remain with this group, he also knew it wasn't the best thing for his family, if they were still alive at all. The time was fast approaching that Gabriel would have to decide between waiting on the group to help him get home, or abandon them and risk going it alone.

***

Jessica

Jessica ran into the room and saw Melissa lying on the bed, clutching her forehead. Lawrence was in the room along with the other active nurse, Kristen. As Jessica stood just inside the room, Melissa looked over at her and smiled.

"Hello, dear," Melissa said.

Jessica, with tears already streaming from her eyes, ran over to the woman. Lawrence moved out of the way, allowing Jessica to reach down and hug the woman with her good arm. She stayed there for at least thirty seconds, crying into the woman's shoulders as Melissa patted her back. With her parents both gone, Melissa was the closest thing Jessica now had to a mother.

Jessica pulled away from Melissa and moved her hair out of her eyes before rubbing the tears away.

"I'm so glad you're okay," Jessica said.

Melissa took the girl's hand and smiled. "Yeah, me too."

"We're going to need to monitor you for a while before we're comfortable with you up walking around," Lawrence said. "We think you suffered some pretty substantial head trauma, but don't think it's permanent. I'm just not sure it would feel too good if you tried to get up and move around."

"I'd really just like to know where I am and what happened."

Jessica told her about the accident, and about how Lawrence had come along, taken out the Empties that had been surrounding them, and brought them here to the hospital. She told Melissa about the place and how it was safe.

"Where's my phone?" Melissa asked.

Jessica shook her head. "It didn't make it here with us," she said.

"Phones aren't working anyways," Sarah added. "They worked for a few seconds the day you guys got here, and then they went down again. Very strange."

Melissa sobbed. "My boy. He's out there somewhere."

"I understand, Mrs. Kessler," Lawrence said. "We all have family out there."

This made Jessica cry again. She thought of her parents lying on the bed and how she no longer had anyone 'out there'. Melissa Kessler and the people in the hospital were now her only family.

Lawrence looked over to the two nurses in the room. "Come on, ladies. Let's let Mrs. Kessler rest and catch up with Ms. Davies, here."

"Thank you, Lawrence," Jessica said.

"No problem." He looked over to Melissa. "Just page us if

you need anything, alright? I'll have someone bring you some food in just a bit."

"That'd be great, thanks," Melissa said, smiling.

Lawrence and the two nurses left the room, leaving Jessica and Melissa alone to talk and be thankful that they were both alive.

CHAPTER THIRTEEN

David

The hallway was empty when David emerged from his room. He was hungry and would eventually go eat, but he wanted to check on something else first. He was barefoot, which allowed him to walk on the tile floor without making enough noise to attract anyone.

He stepped all the way out of the doorway and shut the door behind him, then turned down the hallway, away from the break room. Kristen, one of the nurses, came out of a nearby room, and he smiled at her.

"You going to go eat?" she asked him.

"Yeah, yeah. Just stretching my legs."

"Alright," she replied with a smile. "I'll see you in there."

David reached the end of the hallway. In one direction were the elevators, and to the other were the double doors that led back to the wing of the hospital where only the survivors who worked at the hospital, apparently, were allowed to go.

He looked behind him to make sure that the hallway was clear. When he saw it was, he turned and headed through the double doors, once again ignoring the "Employees Only" sign.

***

The hallways in this wing were still dark. David moved more quickly this time, having already navigated this part of the hospital before. He only slowed down when he came closer to *her*.

Like before, the hallway was dark except for the light coming out of the room that housed the creature. As he reached the corner that led around to the room, he could see the light shining out of the large window. He stepped around the corner and heard the snarls.

David looked into the room, and there was Joanne. Their experiment. It was still lying on the bed, restrained with all the machinery still attached.

As he approached the window, it looked up at him. Its growling became more intense and it tried to fight its way out of the restraints. David looked down at them and noticed that they'd used leather straps, which were locked in tight. Joanne wasn't going anywhere.

He looked around inside the room and noticed a scalpel sitting on a small table. The urge to kill was crawling inside of him again. There was no reason for this creature to be here. They'd already found out that the disease wasn't viral and, as far as he knew, hadn't discovered anything else. If they had, why wouldn't they share it with the other survivors? Joanne... this thing, had served its purpose. He could eliminate it, thus satisfying his hunger to destroy.

David took two steps to his right, never letting his eyes leave those of the creature's. He reached down to open the door, but it was locked. Frustrated, he pulled harder, but it wouldn't open. He slammed his hand against the glass and watched as the Empty tried to raise up, almost as if it were toying with him. David let his forehead rest against the glass and he could feel the sweat drip down his brow.

"So, we meet here once again, Mr. Ellis?"

Startled, David looked over to Lawrence and sighed.

Lawrence approached David. "Why are you here, David?"

"I was just stretching my legs. Thought I'd come take a look at it again." David nodded his head toward the restrained Empty.

"Uh huh, I see."

"Maybe you guys should lock those God damned doors if you don't want people coming back here. Aren't you trying to hide this thing?"

"Most everyone knows about Joanne. I only asked you earlier not to share that you'd been back here because the two women we picked up, Jessica and Melissa, they aren't aware yet."

Lawrence stepped closer to him, and David clenched his fist, not sure what the man's intentions were.

"Humanity is devolving, Mr. Ellis. Just look. Between her and the ones we saw earlier, *this* is what we are becoming. It may take a long time to happen, but it *will* happen."

"Why do you say that?"

"Because, this patient isn't sick. If she's not sick, I'm not sure how she can be cured. And if she can't be cured, then, well..."

David let the words hang in the air, waiting on Lawrence to finish his thought.

"I want to go out again."

David narrowed his eyes. "We just fucking got back."

"I know, David. But aside from bringing back a few sedatives, we didn't find anything. We need to find gasoline. The vehicles are running low, and we have a small emergency generator that runs off fuel as well. Aside from that, I know there are people out there who need our help. That thing I shot that had its hands on you at the clinic... I knew that man. He was my friend, Ray, a great veterinarian. And I fucking shot him."

Lawrence stopped to gather himself.

"We can't let people who need help just die out there when we have a type of sanctuary here."

"Get one of those other guys to go."

Lawrence put his hand on David's shoulder, and David looked down at it before glaring up at the man.

"I saw what you did today. Truth is, I'm not a hundred percent sure that I can trust you yet. But, I need *you* out there with me. Besides, I think you owe me. Twice now, if I remember correct."

David threw the man's hand off his shoulder. "I don't owe you shit." He glared at Lawrence until he'd passed him, and headed for the main part of the hospital they were staying in. "I'll be in my room."

***

Jessica

"No, that's fine, I'll just take water and something small to eat," Melissa said.

Jessica smiled. "Okay. I'll be back in just a few minutes."

"Sounds great."

As Jessica stepped out into the hallway, Lawrence came walking toward her from her right. Though he was wearing long sleeves, Jessica could see the blood stains on his hands, which she hadn't noticed before, and she thought back to her encounter with David in the break room.

Lawrence nodded at her as he approached her. “Jessica.”

Jessica smiled, and as he walked by her, she stopped him. “Wait.”

Lawrence turned around. “Yes?”

She stepped toward him, and looked down at his exposed wrists. He cleared his throat and pulled his sleeves down.

“I want to help,” she said.

“Well, you are helping. I heard you helped out with the laundry earlier, and you’re keeping an eye on Mrs. Kessler.”

Jessica shook her head. “No, I want to go with you.”

“Go with me?”

“On a run.”

Lawrence crossed his arms and smiled with a small laugh. “Jessica, it’s dangerous out there. You don’t...”

“I know what it’s like out there,” Jessica said, cutting him off with frustration in her voice. “You have no idea what we went through, what we saw.”

“Jessica, I almost got killed today.”

“Yeah, and what’s it going to be like around here if that happens? And even if it doesn’t, do you think we can *actually* hold this place forever? Everyone in here needs to be prepared in case something happens and we have to leave, or if we have to defend this place. Does anyone else even know where the weapons are that you have?”

“What I’m trying to do is give everyone here an idea of normalcy. Give them jobs, a purpose, so that they can live normal lives.”

“All you’re doing is distracting them. Everyone needs to know what it’s like out there. The truth.”

Lawrence sighed. “Look, let me think on taking you out

on a run, okay?"

Jessica put her hands on her waist and looked at the wall next to her, exhaling a deep breath. Without looking toward him, she nodded. "Yeah."

"Good," he said, and turned around and walked away from her. "I'll let you know."

Jessica took a deep breath and walked behind him, toward the lounge. Lawrence stopped to speak with Trevor in the hallway, and Jessica continued walking without looking over at them.

***

Lawrence

After speaking with Trevor for a few minutes about a couple of things he'd seen on his latest run, Lawrence retreated to his room. His entire body ached from the events at the animal hospital, and he was exhausted. He walked over to the bed and sat on the edge, kicking his shoes off right as he sat down. He then lay on the bed and felt relief in his back and in his legs.

With his right hand resting on his stomach, Lawrence looked to the ceiling and breathed heavy. In his solitude, his mind naturally went back to his wife and their young son. He looked over at the table by the bed and grabbed the photograph of them at Six Flags.

Lawrence held the photograph up in front of his face, ignoring the soreness in his bicep as he tried to hold the picture steady. It was the only physical photograph he had of them. As he looked into their faces and saw how happy all three of them had been, Lawrence began to cry.

He clutched the photograph to his chest, closed his eyes,

and wept.

***

5 days earlier

The scene at the park was mad. Lawrence had just watched his partner turn into some kind of creature and attack him. Somehow, he'd managed to get away from her. He wanted to try and help her, but when he looked around and saw people being eaten alive, and others running every direction, he decided it best to get the hell out of there.

He ran through all the commotion and reached the ambulance, which they'd kept running. Luckily, no one had jumped inside and driven off with it. All he could think about was Bailey and Carter. He knew they were home, as Bailey was in between jobs, having recently been laid off, and Carter had taken the day off from school because he wasn't feeling well. Lawrence picked up his cell phone and hit the preset number for home as he tried pulling out of the parking lot. People were running all around him, looking as if they didn't know what to do or where to go. The phone rang and rang.

"Come on, pick up the phone, Bailey!"

Lawrence heard a bang on the passenger side door and saw a woman crying through the window. He hit the power locks to unlock the door, and she swung it open.

"Get in!" he yelled.

As the crying woman tried to get into the ambulance, she screamed and was pulled back onto the ground. Someone was on top of her and Lawrence saw the blood begin to squirt from either side. Soon, someone else was on the woman. He looked on with his eyes wide, as one of the sick men came into view and tried to climb into the ambulance. The man's eyes had gone pale and he was spitting toward Lawrence.

Lawrence pressed the gas and watched the man fall away onto the concrete.

All around him, people were screaming. Other cars were leaving, some running into one another and causing wrecks, but Lawrence had avoided having an accident so far.

He made it out onto the road and headed for his house, which was only a couple of miles away from the park.

***

All the way home, the scene was much the same: lots of panic, screaming, wrecks, and lurking sick people. Lawrence continued to try and call home with no luck. He'd also tried to get through to anyone on his CB radio, finally getting through to a fellow paramedic, Chase, who was reporting to him a lot of the same things he was seeing. Lawrence heard a loud crash come through the radio just before losing contact with Chase.

He threw down the radio and focused on getting home.

A few minutes later, he pulled into the parking lot of his apartment complex and weaved his way back to Building 12 where their second-story apartment was.

People out in the parking lot yelled and tried to wave him down, pleading for him to come and help them.

"Oh my God, my child! He's sick!" a woman yelled

"Something bit my mom!" a little boy screamed.

"Please, help me!" another woman pleaded, holding her arm where one of the things had presumably attacked her.

It was difficult, but Lawrence had to ignore all of the requests. Even if he'd wanted to, he couldn't help everyone, and he had his own family to get to.

When Lawrence finally reached Building 12, he shut off the engine and pulled the key out. Before getting out of the ambulance, he reached over to the glove box and pulled out a 9mm he left in there for emergencies.

When his feet hit the parking lot, one of the things immediately reached for him. His eyes went wide as he tried to push it away. It grabbed onto his shoulders and pinned him against the side of the ambulance. Behind it, he watched a woman run by screaming, not even trying to help him. He watched as she ran into one of the creatures, and it took her down to the ground and tore into her.

The thing in front of him was chomping its jaws at him. He finally got the upper hand and turned to pin it against the side of the vehicle.

It worked to try and bite at his fingers, and he was finally able to release its grasp, step back, and draw the gun.

Lawrence fired two shots into the thing's chest, which didn't faze it. The creature came at him again, arms outstretched as if nothing had happened.

Just before it reached him, Lawrence raised the gun and shot at the thing's head. It let out one last snarl as it fell to the ground and went still.

Lawrence turned around and his eyes fixed to the woman who was being eaten on the ground near him. The thing didn't even look away to face him. Though she was long dead, the woman didn't deserve to have her body mutilated any further. He pointed the gun at the back of the head of the beast and pulled the trigger before racing up the stairs to his apartment.

***

Lawrence fumbled with his keys when he reached his apartment. Screams came from his neighbors' units on either side of his, as he finally got the key in the lock and entered his apartment.

When he walked in, the screaming from either wall became more apparent. He could hear banging on the wall from inside of the Davis' place. Mostly drowned out by the screams and the crashing on the walls, John Coltrane's "A Love Supreme" played through a small radio on top of their entertainment center. The living room was exactly as he'd left it that morning, and neither Bailey nor Carter were in there.

"Bailey? Carter?"

He didn't get a response.

As he moved through the large, three-bedroom apartment, he could hear indistinct vocalizing coming from a far room. He passed the kitchen and headed back toward Carter's room. The sound of the quartet coming from the speakers faded, and Lawrence heard some type of groan coming from his son's room.

He approached the door, the gun raised and his heart thudding.

Lawrence lowered the gun as he reached the room. He put his ear to the door and heard the confused noises from the other side. He was trembling and already starting to cry when he reached for the door handle.

He turned. Pulled.

As he looked into the room, his worst dream was realized.

Bailey and Carter were both standing in the middle of the

room, but it wasn't them at all. They were bumping into each other when they looked up toward Lawrence with ghostly eyes. Drool had collected around their mouths and they spat as they lumbered toward him. Lawrence nearly fell down to the ground.

As they had almost made it to the door, Lawrence somehow gathered himself and he slammed the door and put his back to it, sliding down its wooden frame.

Banging erupted behind him, and Lawrence put his head into his knees as he cried out and screamed through the empty apartment.

***

David

After going to check on Joanne, David stopped by the lounge to make himself a quick lunch, heating up a frozen dinner with a small chicken breast, corn, and green beans. He wanted nothing more than to go to his favorite steakhouse back home in St. Louis, but figured that the frozen dinner was maybe a better option than he'd have outside.

He'd come back to his room shortly after, stripped down to his briefs, and decided to lie down for a nap.

Just as David was about to fall asleep, a knock came at the door, and it opened, bringing light from the hallway into the room. *What the fuck?*

He looked up and saw Lawrence in the doorway.

"Ready?"

"Is this your idea of *later*? You've got to be fucking kidding me."

"We need to get this done. I wanna go out while we've got

plenty of daylight."

David sighed. "Give me a few minutes."

"I'll be in the garage."

***

Ten minutes later, David walked through the door into the parking garage. Lawrence was waiting on him inside a four-door sedan that he'd pulled up near the door. He looked over at the ambulance, which was sitting where they'd parked it earlier.

"Not taking the ambulance?" David asked.

Lawrence shook his head. "Nah. Brandon and Trevor are going on a run a little later. Thought I'd let them take it, in case they pick anyone up."

David nodded, opened the door, and got into the car.

Once inside, he peeked into the back seat and saw two rifles sitting on it, as well as four handguns, along with four gas cans each of which would hold five gallons.

Lawrence pulled the vehicle up to the gate and nodded at Sam and Trevor to open it.

As they did, three creatures appeared. Trevor shot two of them with a small handgun, while Sam took down the other with a shotgun.

Lawrence hit the gas, and David looked in the rearview mirror, watching the gate close behind them as they headed out into the world again.

CHAPTER FOURTEEN

Will

When they finally came to the sign that said "Welcome to Knoxville", Will felt as if he could have cried. After fighting their way down the highway for days, they'd made it. Will only hoped that his parents were still around and that they were safe.

"Just keep your eyes peeled," Will said. "Assuming they still have their vehicle, we're looking for a white minivan with South Carolina plates and a bumper sticker that says 'Blessed'."

"Aren't we all?" Marcus asked jokingly, apparently referring to the irony in the bumper sticker.

Will let out a short laugh and then continued to look outside.

Knoxville was the first metro area they'd been in since Nashville, and it amazed him how vacant it was. While there were more abandoned automobiles and Empties out on the road, he'd expected to maybe see more survivors around. It made him wonder just how many people had actually made it.

"We're gonna need to try and get some gas for this thing soon. We should be good for a while longer, but we'll need some sooner than later," Marcus said. The group had found a couple of gas cans at the quick lube shop they stayed at once they escaped Ellis Metals, but they'd already used their contents and refilled them with unleaded fuel; the fire truck ran on diesel.

Will looked back to check on everyone else. The fire truck had enough seats for eight people in the back, and an open space on the floor between the seats. Holly was still lying on the floor, unconscious. Dylan was beside her, patiently waiting for her to wake up. Will could see that, over the past few days, Holly had taken Dylan in like he was her little brother, and that the boy had taken to her fairly quickly. Will knew that Dylan was hurting just as much as he was, wanting her so desperately to awaken.

Gabriel sat upright in one of the seats, rubbing his forehead with his hand.

"How you feeling?" Will asked.

"How do you think? Like shit. My whole body hurts."

"Well, just rest, man. Hopefully we'll find my parents soon and we can figure out what we're gonna do next."

"Yeah, okay."

Gabriel was looking outside, and Will could tell that he had other things on his mind. Instead of digging deeper to see what was going on, he found it best just to leave him alone.

He put his focus back onto the road and finding his parents.

***

Lawrence

Like David, Lawrence was exhausted. He didn't want to go out on another run, but he also couldn't sit around the hospital just thinking about his dead family. Going back out into the world and keeping his mind occupied had won out.

They were heading west on I-40 now looking for gasoline. The ambulance was running low, and they also wanted to fill up a couple of containers they had. Lawrence had already checked many of the gas stations, having made this trip many times over the last few days, and thought they might have a better shot of finding gasoline if they reached the outskirts of town.

"You have family?" Lawrence asked David.

Lawrence took his eyes off the road a couple of times, glancing over and waiting on David to respond. The man was simply staring out the passenger side window with his hand to his chin, rubbing the stubble on his beard.

"Why do you hide the weapons?" David asked, ignoring Lawrence's previous question.

Lawrence cleared his throat. "Well, I'm trying to keep everyone's lives normal. How do you think those nurses would feel if everyone was walking around the hospital carrying a gun? That's not exactly normal."

David looked over to him. "And how do you think those nurses are going to feel when enough of those fucking monsters come up to that shitty gate, bust through, and come inside your little sanctuary?" He looked away from Lawrence again, and went back to scanning the highway.

Lawrence swallowed. This was the second time within a couple of hours that one of the outsiders had questioned his motives. Questioned how he was running things at the hospital.

"The others who have been at the hospital from the beginning know where we keep them. Not everyone *needs* to know."

Instead of responding, David just stared back out his window.

"I respect you, Mr. Ellis, and I'm trying to trust you. I need to know that you believe in what I'm doing and how I'm running things."

David looked at him again. "I don't. Not yet."

Lawrence shook his head and refocused on the road. They were near the outskirts of town in an area where Lawrence hadn't traveled since everything fell. He pulled off onto an exit ramp.

"This is as good a place as any to start."

David kept quiet and to himself as Lawrence turned at the end of the ramp and headed toward a small gas station.

***

David

It was your typical exit off of an interstate in the South. The gas station was surrounded by various fast food joints and a few hotels. There were a few Empties in the parking lot of one of the fast food places across the street from the gas station, but he couldn't see any other creatures lurking. As they pulled into the gas station parking lot, David felt a pang reach up into his stomach and he sighed. *Fucking microwave dinner.*

Lawrence stopped in front of one of the gas pumps. David watched him reach into the back and grab one of the gas cans, a hand gun, and a rifle.

"Doesn't look like there are any creatures around here," Lawrence said. "Can you cover me just in case while I try these gas pumps?"

The feeling in David's stomach came on stronger, and he knew he needed to find somewhere to handle it, fast.

"Actually, I've really got to use the restroom. Think you can handle it for a few?"

"Yeah, just hurry. I don't wanna have to leave you if any of those things show up."

David reached in the back for one of the pistols and also saw a knife lying there. It was the same one he had earlier at the pet hospital. He grabbed it, too.

"Alright, I'll try and hurry."

David opened the door, and jogged to the front of the convenient store.

***

When David reached the front of the gas station convenient store, he noticed the handwritten sign on the door that said "Restrooms At Side of Building" and had an arrow directing him where to go. He looked through the window and saw that the gas station had been completely raided. Seeing this, he assumed Lawrence wouldn't be finding any gas left in those pumps.

As he hurried around the corner to the restroom, he heard snarls. The feeling he'd had earlier crept back up inside him. His need to kill had returned. He snuck around back and saw two Empties chewing at the remains of what looked like it might have been a cat or a dog. One of them looked up and limped toward him.

Not wanting to attract any others, David pulled out the knife and drove it into the thing's head. He felt satisfaction in the kill, especially from doing it by hand with the knife, and feeling the blade slip out of the thing's skull. The slippery wet sound as the knife retracted from the thing's brain excited him.

He walked over to the other Empty, which had remained focused on the animal carcass. It looked up at him, but he was already bringing the knife down into its skull. This time, he didn't stop. He slammed the knife into its head, over and over, until his arm finally tired. He stood upright, breathing heavily as he looked down at the damage he'd done. Blood was all over his fresh shirt and he could feel it running down his face.

Not satisfied, and remembering the feeling he'd had earlier in the day at the animal clinic, David raised his leg and slammed his foot into the thing's skull, permanently fusing the creature's head with the concrete.

***

The restroom still had running water, and David washed the blood off his face and his arms. He still felt a high from the kill, and it had temporarily taken the need to use the restroom out of his stomach.

The feeling soon returned, though, and David sat down on the toilet.

As he sat there, he looked down at his hands. Though he'd just washed them, they were still stained with blood from the massacre earlier in the day, and it brought a smile to his face.

He looked up when he heard a loud engine outside. It sounded as if it had pulled into the gas station, and now the engine held still as it idled.

David finished his business, pulled up his pants, and walked out of the restroom.

He walked around the corner and quickly retreated, standing flat against the wall where no one could see him. *No way.*

David peeked his head around the front of the building and his eyes widened.

"You've got to be shitting me."

Lawrence stood just outside the sedan, talking to Will and Marcus.

Sweat formed on David's brow. He couldn't believe that his traitor former best friend and the asshole he'd had taken hostage—two of the people who'd left him for dead back at his warehouse—were now standing just mere yards away from him. David pulled back, leaning flat against the side of the building where they couldn't see him. He tried to quiet his heavy breathing so he could hear what they were saying, but they weren't close enough for him to make out their words clearly.

He gripped the handle of the knife tight at his hip with his right hand and used his left hand to grasp the handgun. He could feel sweat collect around the grip of the gun, and it almost felt as if it could slip out of his palm. The anticipation inside him grew. He wanted nothing more than to run around the corner and put a bullet into Will's brain, but he had to be patient and smart. He knew they had been heavily armed when they'd left Ellis Metals, and also that it hadn't just been the two of them. David hadn't gotten a look into the fire engine, but he assumed that there were others in there.

Then, David heard footsteps walking toward him. He licked his lips and readied the knife. Whoever came around the corner, he would take great joy in gutting them. He'd cover their mouth, throw them against the wall, and cut them wide open.

Just as David saw a shadow and prepared his attack, a voice stopped the footsteps.

"Gabriel, come back! Holly is waking up!"

The shadow disappeared and David heard the man who must have been Gabriel hurrying back over toward the group.

He decided the best thing would be to wait. Finding a fire truck wouldn't be difficult, and he could devise a better plan to get payback on the group who had left him to die.

David retreated to the bathroom, and waited for the truck to pull away.

***

Lawrence

"You're sure you don't want to come back with us?" Lawrence asked. "We've got a good group and can treat your people's wounds."

Will shook his head. "No, thank you, though. We really need to stay on the road so we can get to the East Coast."

"I understand. I'm sure that boy misses his family."

Will reached out to Lawrence, and Lawrence took his hand and shook it.

"Thank you again for taking a look at Holly," Will said. "And we really do appreciate the offer."

"No problem. Best of luck."

Lawrence watched as Will loaded into the truck with the others, who'd already buckled back into their seats. He waved at them as they pulled away and headed back toward the interstate.

When the truck was almost out of view, he turned when he heard David approaching behind him. Lawrence laughed.

"You alright there?"

David nodded. "Yeah. Just feeling a little ill. I'm not used to eating frozen food. But, I'm better now."

"Good."

"Any luck finding gas?"

Lawrence shook his head. "Empty."

"Damn," David said, scratching his head. "Hey, uh, did I hear someone else up here?"

Lawrence nodded. "Yeah, there was another group here for just a few minutes. I was hoping you'd get to meet them, but they got out of here pretty quick. They're looking for gas, too."

"Hmm. Did they say where they were going?"

"East Coast."

"We haven't seen many survivors. How many of them were there?"

"Five. Three men, a woman, and a kid. Poor damn kid. He got separated from his parents. I guess that's where they're headed... trying to get that boy back to them."

"Yeah, poor kid," David mumbled.

Lawrence was taken aback by David's sudden urge to carry on a conversation. Then, he looked down and noticed David had fresh blood on him, and he pointed to it.

"That's not from earlier. That looks new."

"Yeah. I had a little run in back by the restroom. There were a couple of those things back there."

"Ah. Well, glad you're okay," Lawrence said. "So, uh, you ready to get going and see if we can find some gas?"

David nodded.

The two men loaded into the car, and Lawrence turned out of the gas station and headed away from the interstate.

CHAPTER FIFTEEN

Will

"Why didn't you just tell him the truth?" Gabriel asked Will. Gabriel was in the floor of the back seat, tending to Holly, while Will sat up front, looking for his parents' van.

"Didn't trust him. After all the shit we've been through, it feels pretty difficult to trust *anyone* anymore."

"I don't know, Will," Marcus said. "Sounds like the guy may have had a sweet spot for us to go hang our hats for a bit and regroup. I didn't get the same vibe you got."

"And what about that guy at the pawn shop?" Gabriel asked. "Remember the shitty vibe I had about him?"

"Yeah, and how did he turn out? Who was right about that one?" Will reminded Gabriel.

Gabriel started to bow toward Will, but Holly grabbed him.

"Look guys, it's over," she groaned. "Let's just move on and keep our eyes out for the van, okay?"

Will let out a deep breath and he could tell from the aura in the air that both men were frustrated. They were questioning his decision to not trust the man, which in turn, frustrated him. He decided to let it rest.

While he knew he needed to be looking for his parents' minivan, Will couldn't help but look back at Holly. He was so thankful that she had come out of her sleep. While he'd only known her a few days, he had a connection to her that he couldn't see ever having with anyone else. They'd been through more together than he had ever been with any of his past friends. Each time he looked back at her, she smile at him, bringing him at least *some* comfort.

"I'm glad you're okay," Will said back to her.

"Me, too." She cleared her throat. "So, what happened to Miranda?"

Gabriel retold the story to her just as it had been told to him. Will only had to interrupt one time to correct him.

"Oh, my God," Holly said once Gabriel had finished. "That's horrible."

"Yeah," Will said. "It was."

Will continued to scan the road, hoping that they'd pass by his parents at any moment. There was no guarantee that his mom and dad were even still in Knoxville, and he could only hope that wasn't the case.

***

David

Lawrence had driven them further away from the interstate and they were now approaching a more rural area. Once they were a few miles down the road, they came across another gas station. This one was very old and, though it looked like it had long been closed down, the gas prices posted on the large sign out front signaled that it had recently been open.

"Guess we can give this one a shot," Lawrence said.

As they pulled into the gas station, David could see a large house with a barn near it, just a couple of hundred yards behind the convenient store. Lawrence stopped the car right next to one of the gas pumps.

David stepped out, and he felt the same pain in his stomach that he had before.

"Shit," David said, clutching his stomach.

Lawrence looked over at him. "Again?"

Hunched over, David ran toward the front of the convenience store. This one was much smaller than the last one, and he saw from looking through the window that the bathrooms were inside the store. He reached down to the handle and pulled the door, and to his surprise, it opened.

The various cigarette and beer posters on the front window had blocked him from seeing a lot of the damage on the inside of the store. Like the last stop, this place had obviously been raided, making David think that they'd once again be looking somewhere else for gasoline.

He ran back to the restroom, choosing the men's room even though it didn't matter any more. He dropped his pants and immediately sat down on the toilet.

After a few minutes, he pulled his pants up and walked out the door of the restroom, not bothering to flush the toilet behind him.

As the door opened, he heard yelling outside and ducked down as he saw a group of men talking to Lawrence, who had his hands raised in the air. David crouched down low to where he wouldn't be seen, and made his way to the front of the store. David clutched the gun at his side, then remained still and listened.

"Yes, I'm alone," Lawrence said.

"You better not be fuckin' lyin' to me, nigger." The man had a deep country accent, common to East Tennessee.

"Take the guns. The car. Whatever."

"Oh, you better believe we will." This voice was different.

David's heart was beating rapidly in his chest.

"This shit's gonna serve our camp very well, you better believe it."

"Take whatever you want."

David heard a loud pop and then a slam. He had his back against a wall of shelving that lay against the window, and he peeked through a gap to see outside. Lawrence was on the ground on his hands and knees, holding his jaw.

"Get the fuck up, darky!" one of the other men yelled.

David watched Lawrence stumble to his feet, only to be kicked in the knee and fall again. David counted six men, most of them armed from what he could tell.

One of the men approached Lawrence with a grin. He chuckled, as if toying with Lawrence, then swung his combat boot right into Lawrence's jaw. David looked to the sedan and saw that one of the other men was shuffling through the backseat, pulling out the guns and ammo that Lawrence had placed back there.

The man in the middle of the group approached Lawrence's battered body. He wore a trucker hat and a dirty t-shirt tucked into a pair of faded camouflage cargo pants. He kicked Lawrence, not so hard that it would likely hurt, but enough to where it would be irritating. The man squatted down and slapped Lawrence across the face, again, just enough to annoy him and get his attention.

"Get up," the man commanded in an even tone.

Lawrence barely moved. He looked like he was trying to get up, but just didn't have it in him.

"Get his ass up," the man in the camo pants commanded to the other men. Two of his comrades walked over to Lawrence and grabbed him under the arms, lifting him up to his knees. David could see Lawrence's face clearly while the men held him up. Blood pooled from his mouth and his left eye was already starting to swell. The men had done a real number on him in a short period of time.

The man in the camo pants, who David presumed at this point was the leader of the group, hinged at the hips to get his face closer to Lawrence's, and he lifted the paramedic's chin up.

David could see the man saying something to Lawrence, but he was speaking too softly for him to hear it from inside the convenience store.

Then, the man stood back, pulled a pistol out of his pocket, pressed it against Lawrence's forehead, and pulled the trigger.

The other men cheered, one even firing two shots into the air with his own gun.

The man in the camo pants pushed the guy firing the gun. "Stop that shit! You wanna attract them monsters?"

One of the other men laughed until the man in the camo pants got in his face. "What? You think it's funny?" He was speaking just loudly enough to where David could hear him.

"Clear out the vehicle so we can get the hell out of here."

"I've gotta go inside and take a shit," one of the other men said.

"You can wait."

"I'm not so sure that I can, Clint."

David had to think quickly. If the men came in here,

they'd surely kill him without question. They'd assume that he was friends with the man they'd just murdered in cold blood, then put the cold barrel to his head, as well. Truth be told, they had only saved David the trouble of killing Lawrence. With Lawrence out of the picture, he could run the hospital the way he wanted. No one there would stop him. But none of that mattered if he didn't make it back there alive. Would the rednecks really give him the time to convince them that they had done him a favor if they walked in here and found him?

David decided to take a gamble.

He crawled over to the door and, still using the shelving for cover, reached over and pushed the door open to where it was slightly cracked.

"I can get you more weapons!" David yelled.

"Who the fuck was that?" one of the men yelled.

David heard rapid footsteps coming his way and, before he could shut the front door to the market, the man in the camo pants was over him, pressing the gun against his skull.

CHAPTER SIXTEEN

Jessica

Since Jessica had spent every second with Melissa since the woman had woken up from her coma, Melissa now encouraged her to get out of the room for a little while. At first, Jessica resisted, feeling bad for leaving the new widow alone. But, Melissa persisted, and did all *but* come out and say that she wanted to be by herself for a while.

Jessica walked to the lounge and then to the guest area where she'd gone earlier to do laundry, then decided to go explore parts of the hospital she hadn't been in yet. There wasn't anything else to do after all, so she thought she'd have some time to herself and go have a look around. The few people who were at the hospital weren't roaming the hallways, leaving Jessica alone. She walked down past her room in a direction she hadn't gone yet.

When she reached the end of the hall, she turned and saw a group of elevators. Lawrence had been very clear about not using the elevators, and there were even signs on them to deter anyone from doing so.

Down the other corridor, Jessica saw a set of double doors. She walked over to them and pushed. She was surprised when the doors opened because of the "Employees Only" sign posted on the door. She let go of the doors and started to leave, but changed her mind and headed through them anyway.

***

Gabriel

The cell phone had the same "No Service" message plastered across the top left corner that it had had every time he'd looked at it. Gabriel's frustration was quickly mounting. He'd nearly been killed, again, and still had no way of contacting his family. His couldn't stay still in the seat as his patience continued to deteriorate.

Gabriel looked outside, accustomed to the same scene of abandoned cars and wandering Empties that they'd watched for days. In the front seat, he could see Will leaning on the dash, carefully looking out for a minivan they'd never find. Holly was keeping Dylan occupied, looking through an outdoors enthusiast magazine they'd found in the fire truck. They were apparently playing some sort of game where they were making fun of the people in the photos, but Gabriel didn't really understand what they were laughing at. Seeing the boy happy brought him at least *some* joy, though it made him miss Sarah even more.

He hadn't told the group yet. He knew the time had to be right, especially for Dylan. But he knew, for the sake of his own sanity, it would need to be soon.

Gabriel reached into his pocket and pulled out a balled fist. When he opened his hand, the wing pendant that he'd taken from Captain Savage's dead body lay in his palm. He thought about how lucky he was to be alive and how there had to be a reason for it. He looked over to Dylan. The boy, perhaps he was the reason Gabriel was still alive. Gabriel closed his palm and put the wings back into his pocket, then looked up to the front seat.

"They could be anywhere out here, Will," Gabriel said.

"I know, but I have to look."

"What if they aren't even in Knoxville anymore?"

"They're here."

"But, what if..."

"They're here," Marcus said, glaring at Gabriel through the rearview mirror.

Gabriel sighed and shook his head. "We should've gone to that damn hospital," he mumbled to himself.

How long could they really look for Will's parents? He'd already made the decision to forego the refuge at the hospital that the man at the gas station had offered. Though he'd gotten the group out of some tight spots, that didn't give Will the authority to be solely making such decisions. But, Gabriel didn't fight it. For some reason, Marcus was going along with Will. Maybe it was because he felt bad for the kid.

Besides, Gabriel had his own plans.

Will pointing to the other side of the interstate caught Gabriel's attention, causing him to look up.

"There! Go over there!" Will shouted, nearly standing up on the floorboard.

"What is it?" Holly asked, leaning into the front seat.

"I think that's it!"

Gabriel looked out the window and saw a van sitting just off the side of the road. When he looked back over to Will in the front seat, he saw him covering his mouth, clearly upset. Holly was between the seats, holding Will's hand.

He saw that Dylan was confused. They made eye contact, and when he realized that the boy looked like he was about to say something, Gabriel put his index finger to his lips, and the boy remained quiet.

In the front seat, Will had begun to sob.

And as Marcus drove the truck onto the exit ramp to get to the other side of the interstate, Gabriel decided to keep his news to himself a little while longer.

***

Jessica

The corridor she was walking down was almost pitch black. There was just enough light to where she could see doors on either side of her. It looked similar to the hallway she was living in, and she wondered if Lawrence planned to eventually use this part of the hospital to house more survivors.

She reached a corner, and when she moved around it, she saw a small shine of light at the distant end of another hallway. Something about the darkness and how no one had told her any of this was back here bothered her. She felt as if she shouldn't be back here, which was part of what drove her further down the hallway.

On each side of her, there were more of the same types of rooms. As Jessica approached the end of this hallway, she heard an indistinct noise. Though it sounded vaguely familiar, it was still too far off for her to know exactly what it was.

Jessica came to the corner and saw the light bleeding out into the next hallway around the corner.

And the noise she heard was much clearer.

No.

Her breathing was heavy. She felt the sweat trickle down

her cheek. Her heartbeat picked up the pace.

Jessica closed her eyes as she moved around the corner and, when she opened them again, she saw it.

“Oh, my God.”

***

Will

Before the fire engine had even come to a stop, Will jumped out onto the concrete and almost fell down, but managed to catch himself with his hand. He ignored the burning in his palm and ran to the van.

He stopped a car-length away and put his hands behind his head, breathing heavy.

A gunshot rang through the air and Will jumped. He turned around and saw Marcus holding a rifle up to his shoulder. Will had been so taken aback by finding his parents’ van that he hadn’t even noticed the Empty that had been coming at him.

Marcus ran up to him and put his hand on Will’s shoulder. “I know you’re upset by this, but you’ve got to look the fuck out!” Marcus scanned the area. “It looks like that’s the only one. We should be clear.”

Will sobbed more than before. “This is it, Marcus. This is their van. It’s their fucking van!”

Will could hear more footsteps come up from behind him, but he didn’t turn around. He felt an embrace. Holly wrapped her arm around him, resting her head on his shoulder and rubbing his chest with her other hand. She was also crying, though not as intensely as he was.

Marcus pulled away and slowly walked forward. Will realized he hadn’t even checked inside yet. What if they were in there? He couldn't bear the thought of seeing his parents lying in there dead. And what if the Empties had gotten to them? Worse yet, what if *they* had turned into Empties?

Will watched Marcus peek over the side of the van to look inside. Will's heart punched his ribcage. Holly held him tighter, as he waited for Marcus to give him a signal one way or the other.

Marcus looked up and shook his head.

"What? What does that mean?" Will asked.

"No one's in there."

Will sighed. While he'd still lost hope, at least he didn't have to look at his parents inside the van, either dead or turned into Empties.

"I'm never gonna see them again," Will mumbled, trying to talk clearly through the sniffles.

"Don't say that, sweetie. You don't know that," Holly replied.

Will pulled away from her and pointed at the van. "Look at this, Holly! Who's to say they didn't get thrown from the van and Empties got them? They could be lying in that tall grass over there!" Will was pointing toward the tall straw grass that started about ten yards away from where the vehicle lay.

He heard more footsteps behind him and turned to see Gabriel walking toward the grass. Dylan was still standing by the fire truck, and he began to cry as well.

Just as Gabriel and Marcus made it to the grass, they turned their heads. Will heard the noise, too, and then turned around as well.

He made a visor with his hand to protect his eyes from

the sun and saw the ambulance driving down the highway, heading West toward them.

"Shit," Marcus said. He hurried over to Will and Holly. "Come on, we need to get back in the truck."

Will agreed. They couldn't let the fact that it was an ambulance coming toward them cloud their judgment. They had to be cautious, as they didn't know who was inside. The group had made an agreement to be wary of anyone they saw, because they assumed that people were now just as desperate as they were. It was partly why Will had had a bad feeling about the man at the gas station; he just didn't trust him.

Sitting in the front seat on the passenger side, Will looked over into the driver's side mirror and saw the ambulance steadily approaching. He kept a tight grip on his handgun, anticipating the ambulance's stop.

As predicted, the ambulance came to a halt next to the fire truck. The man in the passenger side was smiling as he rolled the window down.

"Well, looks like we almost got ourselves a whole team. Just need a squad car with some blue lights," the man said, chuckling.

"No shit," Marcus replied, returning a laugh which Will could easily tell was fake.

"What are you folks doing out here?" the driver asked.

Will gripped the gun even tighter now.

"Surviving," Marcus said.

"I hear that," the man said.

"Something doesn't feel right," Holly whispered. Will waved his hand toward her where the men couldn't see it, urging her to stay back and be quiet. Will thought it best that the men didn't know how many people were in the truck, just in case they tried something.

"Say, why were you guys checking out that minivan?" the man in the passenger seat asked.

"None of your fucking business, asshole," Will said with a firmness in his voice.

The man put his hands up. "Whoa, easy there, killer. It's just coincidental, that's all."

"Why is that?" Marcus asked.

"Because I helped rescue the people that were inside it."

Everyone in the truck turned to look at Will, whose eyes had gone wide. He was hyperventilating. The gun slipped out of his hand and hit the floorboard, and it didn't even faze him.

"Everything okay?" the man in the passenger side asked.

"We need you to take us to them," Marcus said. "This man is their son."

CHAPTER SEVENTEEN

David

One of the men picked David up by his shirt collar and dragged him outside into the parking lot of the gas station. They took him back to the vehicle and slammed him up against it. The man in the camo pants stood in front of him now, while the other man kept David pinned against the car. Now, the man had the same gun he'd killed Lawrence with pressed against David's cheek.

"You're about to end up like your dark friend down there, partner," the man said.

"That asshole isn't my friend," David replied.

"Bullshit," one of the other men said.

The man in the camo pants nodded and said, "Yeah, bullshit. You probably went in there to take a shit while he was out here trying to get gasoline."

"Exactly," David said. "I was with him, sure, but that doesn't make him my friend."

"And why should I believe you?" The man pressed his forearm into David's neck, suffocating him.

"There's a hospital," David said, struggling to breathe. "I can take you there. Lots more weapons. Not only weapons, but medical supplies and food as well."

The man let up on David's throat and took a couple of steps back, keeping the gun pointed at his head. One of the other men walked up and whispered something into the leader's cupped ear. The man left his face neutral, and David had no idea if he was about to die or if he'd live at least a little bit longer. A smile came across the man's face and then he lowered the gun.

"Alright. We wanna see this hospital you're talking about. If you're not lyin', then maybe I won't kill ya. But, if you are..."

The man looked down at Lawrence's dead body and spat on it.

"Then you'll end up like your friend down there."

David took two steps toward the man and narrowed his eyes. One of the other men started to move toward David, but the man in the camouflage pants stopped him with his hand.

"For the last time, that son of a bitch isn't my friend. But, if you want us to get into those guns, I suggest you dig through his pocket and find his keys."

***

Will

The man who had been in the passenger seat of the ambulance introduced himself to the group as Brandon. He told them that he worked at a nearby hospital, and confirmed that he knew the black man they'd run into at the gas station when Gabriel asked him about him.

"I need you to take me to my parents," Will told the two men.

The two men looked at each other for a moment, then looked back at Will.

"What?" Will asked.

"Are you sure this is their van?" Trevor, the man who had been driving, asked.

"Absolutely. That's their license plate and everything. My father is bald on top and has gray hair around the side of his head. He always dresses like a goofball. My mom is a little shorter and has dark hair. Her name is—"

"Melissa?" Brandon asked, cutting him off.

"Yes," Will said, breathing heavy now.

"She's at the hospital," Trevor said.

A big smile came across Will's face. "You have to take me there, now! Let's go!"

Will turned around and headed for the passenger side door to the fire truck.

"We only picked up her and a girl," Brandon said.

Will stopped, standing still at the front of the fire truck. He could feel everyone's eyes focused on him, though he couldn't see them.

"Your father wasn't with them."

Will looked up to the sky. Clouds were creeping across the sky, beginning to block out the sun. They started to look like they were speeding up, and Will was becoming dizzy.

"Will?" Holly said from behind him.

Will fell to his knees, continuing to look to the sky. He grabbed onto his hair and screamed as loud as he could as dark clouds came to a halt in front of the sun.

***

Gabriel

The loud cry from Will had attracted a couple of Empties, which Brandon and Trevor volunteered to take care of. After leading Dylan back into the fire truck where he would be safe, Gabriel returned and joined Marcus at the opposite shoulder of the highway. The two men looked on as Holly tried to calm and comfort Will.

After swiftly taking out the two Empties with knives, the two men approached Gabriel and Marcus. Gabriel watched Trevor pull a pack of cigarettes out of his pocket, take one out, and light it.

"Mind if I bum one?" Gabriel asked.

"Sure thing." Trevor handed Gabriel a cigarette, and cupped the lighter as he lit it for him.

"Thanks."

Marcus looked over to Gabriel and chuckled. "You smoke?"

Gabriel inhaled deeply, then pushed the smoke out of his lungs and into the gray sky. "I do now."

Marcus shook his head.

"You guys give us a second?" Gabriel asked, looking toward Trevor and Brandon.

"No problem," Trevor said as he took a drag off the smoke. The two men walked to the ambulance and got inside.

Marcus turned to face Gabriel. "What's up?"

Gabriel took a drag off his cigarette and made a whistling sound as he exhaled.

"I'm leaving."

"What do you mean 'you're leaving'?"

"I mean I'm leaving. I'll go to the hospital with you guys because I want to see that you all get there safe. Then, I'm gonna take Dylan and we're going to drive home to D.C."

Marcus put his hands on his hips and took in a deep

breath, catching some of the cigarette smoke as he did, and waving his hand in front of his face to shoo it away.

"Sorry," Gabriel said, and he threw the half-burned cigarette onto the ground and stomped it out.

"Look, man, I know that you want to get to your family. But, you guys will never make it alone. Besides, it sounds like they've got a real sweet set-up at this hospital. You've got to think about that boy and keeping him safe."

Gabriel moved closer to Marcus and narrowed his eyes. "Aside from my own daughter and my wife, keeping that boy safe is *all* I think about. Don't you question that."

"Then you'd take him to that hospital, away from all this shit."

"And what about his parents? You don't think they're wondering where their child is?"

"It's not going to matter if you can't get him there alive. And for all you know, his God damn parents might be dead!"

Gabriel heard sniffling, and he looked over to see Dylan now standing outside of the fire truck, looking over at them. While Gabriel wasn't sure how long he'd been standing there, he assumed from the boy's reaction that he knew Gabriel was thinking about leaving the group. Tears ran down the child's face, and he turned and ran back up into the fire truck.

Holly was looking back over to them, shaking her head. She looked down and said something to Will, gave him a kiss on the cheek, and then went inside the fire truck with Dylan.

Marcus and Gabriel sighed simultaneously as they kept their eyes toward the fire truck.

"Look," Marcus said to Gabriel, not looking over to him. "Just think about it, okay? Consider all the options."

Gabriel looked over to him. "I have." He kept his eyes on Marcus for another moment as he walked back toward the fire truck.

***

Will

The anticipation crawled around inside of Will. He was finally going to see his mother, but was dreading asking her why his father wasn't with her. He didn't want to ask the question, but knew it would be the first thing out of his mouth once he saw her.

"We're almost there," Trevor told them through the ambulance's CB radio. "That truck isn't going to get inside the garage, and we've got to get to the top level. You'll need to park it and have everyone hop in the back of this. There will probably be creatures walking around, but we'll help cover you, over."

"Sounds good, over," Marcus replied.

A few minutes later, the large hospital came into view. Will's heart raced again. *My mother is inside that building.*

The ambulance pulled up to the entrance of the parking garage, and Will watched four Empties begin to walk from the side of the building to the two vehicles.

"You'll need to hand your weapons over to us once we get inside," Trevor said.

"What?" Holly said from the back seat.

"No way," Gabriel added.

Will and Marcus looked at each other.

"Are you there?" Trevor asked.

"Why do we have to give you our weapons?" Marcus asked.

"Sorry, man. Just the way we do things. We'll cover you."

The Empties were approaching, and Brandon got out and knelt down behind the ambulance, propping the rifle up on the hood of the vehicle. The group sat in the fire truck, staring at each other.

"You coming, or not?" Trevor asked.

"This doesn't feel right," Holly said.

"I agree," Marcus added, holding his thumb just over the button on the radio.

"Hello?" Trevor said through he radio.

"Come on, guys," Dylan said.

Gabriel sighed. "Dylan, we can't just—"

"Yes, we can. Something feels right with them."

While it was hard to trust the instinct of the child, Will agreed with him. His vibe about the two men had changed.

"Let's just do it," Will said.

"Shit," Marcus said. "Alright."

Will had succumbed to the men's demands, and only hoped that his newfound trust for them was warranted.

"Ready?" Will asked. Everyone nodded almost simultaneously, and Will looked over to Marcus.

Marcus pressed the button on the CB. "Here we go."

And with Gabriel going first, the group raced to the ambulance as gunshots sounded all around them.

***

Jessica

No one was in the laundry room, and it made a perfect place for Jessica to go to gather her thoughts. She sat on the floor in the corner of the room, with her knees up to her chest.

The only thing she could think about was the creature in the back of the building. She didn't understand it. For one, why was it even here? Yes, it was restrained and left inside a seemingly secure room, but she didn't expect she would sleep easy knowing the thing was back there. And what did they know about it, if anything? The fact that no one had told her the creature was back there left her uneasy.

After a few minutes of thinking about the creature and questions she'd have for Lawrence whenever he made it back to the hospital, her thoughts returned to her parents. While Jessica knew that she would think about her mom and dad every day for the rest of her life, she hoped that the day would eventually come when she'd be able to remember her parents in more positive and loving thoughts. For the last few days, her mind had only flashed images of the two of them lying on the bed with blood all around them. And now, in a moment of quiet solitude, she was able to let it all out again, shedding tears down onto the tile floor beneath her. The thing that bothered her the most was why her parents had given up so quickly. Though the streets of her old neighborhood had been occupied with dozens of the creatures, the house had been clear of them. It's almost like they'd seen what was going on outside and just decided not to even try. Like they maybe had other things hurting them in their lives that Jessica didn't know about. And it hurt her all the same that she'd now never know.

Jessica looked up when she suddenly heard voices out in the main hallway of the hospital. She got to her feet and pushed through the double doors, into the small administrative area that the laundry room was a part of. As she reached the exit, the sound of footsteps on the tile floor became louder. She opened the door and stepped out into the hallway, and saw unfamiliar figures walking toward her room. Trevor was at the back of the group and looked over at her as she made her way toward him.

She saw Brandon leading the group into Melissa's room and started to run over, but Trevor grabbed her. She looked at him with a confused glare.

"It's okay," he said.

"Who the hell are those people?"

"Oh, my God!" The voice was Melissa's from inside the room.

Jessica pushed Trevor off of her and ran to the room.

She pushed through the group, including Brandon, who was standing just inside the doorway.

Jessica stood still as she entered the room and saw a man leaning over the bed and hugging Melissa. The widow was sobbing uncontrollably, holding onto him as tightly as she could. Melissa's cheek pressed against the man's chest, and her eyes met Jessica's. Jessica could now see that she was smiling. Melissa pulled away from the man and wiped her runny nose, clearing the tears from her eyes.

For the first time, Jessica saw the man's face. He looked around her age, was handsome with dark blondish hair and a scruffy beard, and he was also crying.

"Jessica," Melissa said, grabbing the girl's attention. "This is Will... my son."

***

Will

Everyone was out of the room except the woman who'd

barged in just after Will had entered. She had almost exited when Melissa stopped her.

"Jessica, please stay," Will's mother said.

Will watched the girl turn around and then just stand there. He hadn't been expecting the girl who was with his mother to be so attractive, and he smiled at her.

"Please, close the door and sit down with us," Melissa said.

Jessica closed the door and then sat in a chair at the foot of the bed, while he was sitting at the head of the bed, holding his mother's hand.

Melissa looked down at Jessica and smiled. "Will, this is Jessica. Jessica, this is my son, Will."

Though it was obvious at this point who Will was, the girl still smiled at him, a gesture which he returned.

"I asked Jessica to stay because her story is very important to telling you about your father."

"What about Dad?" Will asked.

Melissa sighed. "Just listen, son."

Will listened as his mother told him everything. She started from the time they checked into the hotel and met Jessica, told him about how his father had saved the girl when she was stuck in the hallway, and how he was bitten trying to get to the elevator. Every now and then, Jessica chimed in, and she ended up having to tell Will the majority of the story that came after his father had been bitten. While it wasn't easy for Jessica, Melissa couldn't make it through telling Will about the final moments at the gas station.

When the women were done, Will just sat there. He still had a hold of his mother's hand, but he didn't say anything.

His eyes filled until he finally broke down, put his head to his mother's hand, and sobbed.

His father was gone. Not only was he gone, but his mother had had to see him turned into an Empty. That was the most difficult part for him to grasp.

After a couple of minutes, he looked up and wiped his eyes. He looked over to Jessica, who had also been crying.

"Thank you, Jessica, so much," Will said.

"Your father saved my life. I'll be forever grateful for that."

Will nodded. "Yeah, but, you've been here for my mom. Doesn't sound like she would have made it here if it weren't for you."

"Yeah, well, your mother was a big help to me, too."

"Would you mind if we had a few minutes alone now, Jessica?" Melissa asked.

Jessica wiped her eyes. "No, of course not." She got up and left the room.

Will leaned in and hugged his mother, and they both continued to cry as Jessica shut the door behind her.

CHAPTER EIGHTEEN

David

Two of Clint's men loaded into the vehicle with David. The man in the camouflage cargo pants had instructed them go to the hospital with David to get the weapons that he claimed were hidden there somewhere. They patted David down, making sure he didn't have any knives or firearms hidden somewhere on his body, and pushed him into the driver's seat.

One of the men sat in the front seat, and the other sat in the back with a shotgun fixed at his hip, clearly fixed toward David. If David made one wrong move, the man could easily blow a hole through the back of the seat and kill him. The man in the front also held a gun, keeping his finger on the trigger of the pistol and the barrel pointed toward David. This man, who wore a white t-shirt and a pair of dirty jeans, and had a goatee and mustache on his face, whistled as he watched outside, glaring over at David from time to time.

"You know, you don't have to keep those guns pointed at me," David said.

The man in the back seat scoffed. "Yeah, okay."

David shook his head.

"Just drive, asshole," the man in the front seat added.

They were just a few miles from the hospital now, and David did just as the man asked and kept moving.

"Felt good to kill your friend back there," the man in the back seat said. "I only wish I had got to do it instead of Clint."

"I bet it did feel good," David said, looking at the man in the rearview mirror.

"You're not gonna fool us and try to make us think you're on our side," the man beside David said. "We know you were friends with that nigger."

David chuckled. "You don't know shit." He waited for one of the men to hit him, but it never happened.

"You got a lot of balls for a dead man," the man in the passenger seat continued. "What's your name anyhow?"

"David."

"Well, David, I'm Trent. And this fella back here, his name is Cody. You just do as we tell you, and we'll make this whole experience a lot less painful for ya. You got that?'

David hesitated, not sure how to respond. He felt like his stiff attitude might be getting through to the men, so he kept it going.

"Yeah, whatever. You do what you gotta do. But, if you kill me, you're making a grave fucking mistake."

"Yeah?" Cody asked from the back seat. "And why's that?"

"Because I can help you with more than getting you some fucking guns."

"And how the fuck can you help us?" Trent asked.

David pointed outside. "I survived two days out there, alone. And that's after being left to die in a fucking warehouse surrounded by those things outside. You got anyone who's done that?"

Trent and Cody were silent.

"Yeah, that's what I thought. And, just so you know, I almost killed that piece of shit earlier today, but one of those things attacked me right before I could get the shot off. I was planning on taking over this damn hospital, soon. Guy you shot was a weak leader, not worth trusting for shit."

"And you *can* be?" Trent asked.

"I didn't say that, did I?"

"Well, what are you saying, then?"

"I'll help you get the guns from this place, but before you kill me, you should let me have another chat with Clint."

Trent looked back to Cody, and David saw Cody shrug in the rearview mirror. Then, Trent looked back over to David.

"You just get us what we need, okay?"

They passed over a hill and the top of the hospital came into view.

Trent pulled the two-way radio from his waistband. It would be the only way for him and Cody to communicate with their camp.

"Clint, you there?"

"Yeah," the man said through the radio.

"We can see the hospital."

***

Gabriel

While the others conversed in the break room, Gabriel sat up against a wall in the hallway. The group had decided to give Will some time alone with his mother, and the survivors in the hospital had offered food to Gabriel's group. While he was hungry, he had too many things on his mind for him to want to be around the others right now.

He had Will's cellphone in his pocket and pulled it out to

try yet again to reach his family. Gabriel pressed down the power button and waited for it to turn on. When it did, he saw on the screen that there was no service, just like every other time he'd looked, but dialed anyway.

And like every other time, nothing happened.

Across from him was a welcome counter for people visiting the hospital. Gabriel stood up and walked to it. He saw a phone on the desk and picked it up, but the line was dead.

Gripping his hair with his fingers, Gabriel worked to hold in his frustration. When he closed his eyes, he saw his daughter as one of *them*, just as she had been in his dream earlier, and it set him over the edge.

Gabriel grabbed the phone with both hands and threw it against the wall. He then knocked the computer off of the desk, sending it crashing to the floor.

The group emerged from the kitchen, but Gabriel continued his enraged destruction of the desk, throwing all its contents off and onto the ground.

"Gabriel!" Marcus yelled.

He ran over to Gabriel and grabbed him. Gabriel pushed him off, and then just looked over to him, breathing heavy.

"Calm down, bro," Marcus said in a more even tone. "What's the matter, Gabriel? Talk to me."

As everyone looked on, Gabriel walked over and hugged Marcus, crying into his shoulder.

***

"Are you sure this is what you want, man?" Will asked Gabriel. He'd come out of his mother's room when he heard the crash down the hallway.

"It's what I want," Gabriel replied.

Marcus, Holly, and Rachel, one of the survivors from the hospital, were there as well.

"What about Dylan? Can you keep him safe by yourself?" Holly asked.

"I did before I met you guys. I don't see why I can't now."

"D.C. is a long way to go," Marcus said.

"I know. But I have to try."

"Don't you wanna wait here a little bit longer? Get your head straight and make sure it's the right decision?" Holly asked.

Before Gabriel could answer, Will did for him.

"No," Will said. "He has to go, and he has to take Dylan. If anyone here gets it, it's me. I know the feeling of finding someone you love in all this mess." Will looked at Gabriel. "I get it, man. You gotta go."

Gabriel nodded.

"We should be able to spare a vehicle for you," Rachel said. "Also, I'll throw you some food. I can't let that boy go without knowing that he won't have something to eat."

"Thank you," Gabriel said. He stood up. "I'm going to go let Dylan know so that you guys can say your goodbyes."

"You're leaving now?" Holly asked.

Gabriel nodded, and headed for the kitchen to get the boy.

***

David

Across the street from the hospital, David Ellis came to a stop.

"Go ahead and pull up in there," Trent said.

David could feel the fire creep up inside him and he couldn't believe his eyes. Parked at the entrance to the multi-level parking garage was the fire truck he'd seen at the gas station earlier. He could see the number "14" emblazoned on its sides, and knew for sure that it was the same one. He swallowed the lump in his throat and gripped the steering wheel tightly, his palms beginning to sweat.

"We can't," David mumbled.

"What the fuck you mean 'we can't'?"

David pointed toward the fire truck. "I know those people. They're the ones who left me for dead back in Nashville."

"So the fuck what?" Cody said from the back seat. "All the more reason for us to go in there and fuck 'em up."

Shaking his head, David said, "It's not that simple. I wish it was, 'cause I'd blow every one of their God damned brains out. But, they'll be armed."

The two men looked at each other, and David looked in the rearview mirror to see Cody nod at Trent.

Trent pulled his gun back out and pressed it right against David's temple.

"You playin' us here?"

"What?" David asked.

Trent leaned toward David and punched his face. David spat toward the window and held his mouth. When he pulled his hand away, blood was on his palm. Trent pressed the barrel back against David's head. In the back seat, Cody had the shotgun pointed toward David again.

"Did you set this shit up? Tell them to come here?"

David laughed. He touched his hand to his mouth again,

feeling the wet blood around his lips. When he saw Trent take his eyes off of him again to look back at Cody, he saw his chance.

David swiped the handgun out of Trent's hand and grabbed the man's arm, holding him in the best armlock he could in the small space. It was effective, as Trent cried out. David pressed the gun against Trent's temple and looked back at Cody, who was trembling there with the shotgun in his hands.

"Put it down!" David demanded.

Cody just sat there, stunned.

David cocked the hammer. "Put the God damn shotgun down, or I swear to Christ, I'll blow his brains out!"

Out of the corner of his eye, David could see Trent nodding toward Cody.

"Put it the fuck down!" Trent pleaded with a tremble in his voice.

The redneck abided, setting the shotgun down in the floorboard behind the passenger seat.

"Now, listen to me you East Tennessee hillbilly fucks," David started. "I've about had it with your shit, okay? I can't begin to tell you how bad I want to kill the assholes who, by the looks of it, I can assume are inside that hospital. I'm not sure how many ways I can tell you that. I'm going to put down this gun, but here is what I want. Are you going to listen?"

David waited for each man to acknowledge that they heard him, then continued.

"We're going to do this smart. We can't barge in there with the few weapons we've got. I know what they are packin', and it's not light. So, we're going to drive a mile or so away and think this through. Probably gonna need to get on that radio and get some back-up."

He cleared his throat before he continued.

"When we're done with all this, I want a meeting with Clint. I'm not gonna wander around out here alone anymore and I'm sure as fuck not gonna let you pricks kill me. I want to become a part of your community, and help you survive. Understand?"

"Y-y-yes," Trent said.

Cody nodded.

"Alright, then," David said. He pulled the pistol away from Trent's head. The man gasped, catching his breath. David turned the gun around, holding it by the barrel, and handed it back to Trent.

Reluctantly, Trent put out his hand and took the weapon. It was a risk for David, but he knew that he'd gotten his point across and felt that he had gained their trust.

"So, what are we gonna do?" Cody asked.

Before David could answer, he looked over toward the parking garage. A red Ford Escape was pulling out and appeared to have two figures inside. When he squinted his eyes, he saw a man and what looked like a child in the front seat.

A smile came across David Ellis' face.

He put the car into drive, and followed the small red SUV.

***

Gabriel

Clouds were forming in the sky, again signaling rain. To Gabriel Alexander, it seemed fitting. He and the boy were alone once again, and he felt as if it made for a much darker road ahead, but one that he needed to travel. There was no way he could go another moment without trying to get home to his wife and daughter and, though it had been a difficult decision, he felt as if he'd left the hospital with Will and the group fully understanding why he had to leave.

Dylan was a different situation.

The boy had stopped sobbing, but sat in the passenger seat in utter silence. Gabriel took his eyes off the road every now and then to look over at the boy, and could see how red his eyes and face were from crying. After a few glances, Dylan turned his head where Gabriel couldn't see his face any longer.

Gabriel sighed and shook his head. He knew that leaving the group was hard on the boy, but also knew that the feeling would pass. There was no way he could leave him behind with Dylan's home being so close to his own. Whether the child liked it or not, he needed to be back home with his parents who, if still alive, were sure to be worried sick about him.

There was a bag in the back seat with some food in it that Rachel had given them. Gabriel reached into the back and grabbed a sandwich that was wrapped in a plastic bag, and offered it to Dylan.

"Hungry?"

Dylan didn't respond.

Again, Gabriel sighed. While he knew the boy would eventually talk again, his patience with Dylan was already starting to wear thin. More than his patience, it was his guilt he couldn't ignore.

"Come on, Dylan. You can't do this forever. At least eat this sandwich."

He was watching the road, but felt the sandwich get snatched out of his hand. Gabriel looked over and, before he could react, Dylan had lowered the window and thrown the sandwich outside.

Gabriel made sure there was no immediate threat of Empties around and then he slammed on the brakes.

The force caused Dylan to lean forward and scream, and his body whiplashed and slammed against the seat as the car came to a stop. Gabriel watched the boy look up at him, crying again.

"Look!" Gabriel started. "I know you hate this. I know that you got close to Holly and Will and Marcus. I get it. I liked them, too. But we couldn't stay with them."

"But why?"

"Because, I have a wife and daughter at home that I have to get to, and your parents have to be worried sick about you. The longer we wait, the more of a chance that we never find them."

Dylan's face changed from sorrow to pure anger. "You don't get it, do you? I hate them! I hate my mom and dad! I hope that they're dead!"

Gabriel's mouth opened and he leaned back against the door. As the parent of a child similar in age, it was extremely difficult for him to hear. He watched as Dylan worked to open the door and leave. Luckily, the child safety lock feature on the vehicle was engaged, leaving Dylan unable to get out. The boy started to bang on the glass.

"Let me out of here!"

"Dylan," Gabriel said, reaching over to try and hug the boy. Dylan fought it at first, but then embraced Gabriel and started to sob into his shoulder.

"I don't want to go home. Please, don't take me there. Just either take me back to the hospital or let me stay with you."

Rubbing the boy's back, Gabriel said, "Alright, alright. Don't worry, I won't take you back home." But what Gabriel wasn't sure about was if he was telling the truth or not.

***

A few minutes later, Gabriel saw a gas station and decided to pull in and try to find some fuel to fill the tank with. They had about a quarter of a tank, but he feared that once they got all the way out of Knoxville, it may be a while before they saw another station. He only hoped that this one would have some gasoline.

As they pulled up closer, he saw that there were three Empties in the parking lot, but he still decided to stop, as they seemed to be the only threat lurking in the area.

"Hang on!" Gabriel told Dylan.

He pulled the car into the gas station parking lot and slammed on the brakes, turning the car around to where the back end faced the front of the store, wanting to avoid a collision with the vehicle's engine. He watched in the rearview mirror as two of the Empties grouped together and headed for the vehicle. Gabriel threw the car into reverse and punched the gas. He yelled out as the rear bumper of the car made contact with the two creatures, sending them to the ground. The car ran over them and he could hear their bodies crush beneath them in the process.

When the two beasts came back into view, Gabriel leaned over the dash and saw that neither of them were moving. He noticed a third Empty approaching the car, arms outstretched, aiming to come at Dylan's window. The boy was breathing heavy, screaming out Gabriel's name for him to do something.

Gabriel looked at the back seat and saw the baseball bat lying on it. He reached back and grabbed it, then got out and walked around the car.

The Empty turned its attention to Gabriel, who was coming around to the hood of the sedan. He had the bat down at his side, but raised it onto his shoulder, preparing to swing at the creature.

"Come on, you son of a bitch," Gabriel mumbled toward the thing.

The Empty snarled and spit at Gabriel.

As it came within a few feet of him, Gabriel reared back and swung the bat with a grunt, connecting with the side of the thing's skull. It had been a little while since he last took one of them down, and it felt good. He stood over the beast and, grabbing the bat by the top, drove the butt end down into the creature's face like a stake. Blood splattered from the ground as the thing's head molded into the concrete.

When he looked back to the car, he saw Dylan watching him. Gabriel thought back to days earlier when this same child had had to kill one of the creatures himself in self-defense. It had crushed the boy. Now, the boy had no emotion whatsoever on his face. In just days, Dylan had adapted to the cold ways of the new world.

Gabriel stood up straight and walked over to the car,

tossed the bloody bat into the back, and got back in. He didn't say a word to Dylan as he put the car into drive and moved it next to one of the gas pumps close to the front of the convenience store.

As he put the car into park, Gabriel set his head back against the seat and let out a deep breath. After a few moments, he looked over to Dylan, who still expressed no emotion on his face. Gabriel cracked a small smile and ran his hand over the boy's head, which had a hat sitting on it.

"Come on, let's go inside for a minute."

Gabriel made sure he had the pistol on his waist that they gave him at the hospital, then stepped out of the car and met the boy on the other side. He took Dylan's hand, and they headed inside.

CHAPTER NINETEEN

Dylan

The inside of the convenience store was trashed. Most of the display racks were completely emptied and left scattered on the floor. Dylan scanned the ground, hoping to maybe at least find a candy bar, but it didn't appear that he was going to have much luck.

Gabriel led him over near the restroom and then leaned down to his face.

"I've got to use the bathroom, okay?" Gabriel said.

Dylan nodded. "Okay."

"I want you to wait right here. You have the gun I gave you, right?"

Again, Dylan nodded, and he patted his right hip.

"Good. Just stay right here. I'll only be a few minutes."

"Okay."

Gabriel smiled down at him and then stood up straight and opened the door to the bathroom, closing it behind him. Dylan heard the faint sound of the fan inside and then he stood there, just as Gabriel had asked.

He scanned the ground again, still hoping to find some candy. While he didn't see any, he did see something else that piqued his interest.

On the ground near the window, a magazine rack had tipped over. He walked over to it and saw the various magazines spread across the floor. He flipped through them, and a big smile came across his face when he saw one of his favorite comic books.

When he picked it up, there was a magazine just below it that had a black cover on it. He grabbed the magazine and ripped the plastic open. A look of surprise came across his face when he saw the naked woman and read "Playboy" across the top. He'd never seen a naked woman before, and knew that his parents would kill him if they knew he had this in his hand. But they weren't around to ground him, were they? He opened up the magazine and let out a giggle at what he saw, then quickly closed it. He didn't think there was any way that Gabriel would let him keep it, and he'd left his bag in the car. Dylan licked his lips and slowly crept toward the door.

Dylan opened the front door to the store, careful to make sure that it didn't make any noise when it shut. He didn't want to startle Gabriel into thinking something was wrong. He hurried over to the car and opened the door to the back seat. He reached over and grabbed his backpack, unzipping the main compartment and slipping in three comic books he'd found that he liked, as well as the Playboy.

He zipped up the bag, and as he was just about to turn around and shut the door, a hand came around his belly and another covered his mouth. He tried to scream, but it was muffled by the palm over his mouth.

Dylan's feet left the concrete and he was turned around. Two men were standing in front of him, one of who had a gun pointed at the boy.

"Hey, kid," the man said in a Southern drawl.

Dylan flailed his arms and legs, and the man holding him picked him up and forced him back inside the convenience store.

***

Gabriel

Gabriel was almost finished when he heard the front door to the convenience store open. He looked up from the ground and his hand immediately went to his holster and grabbed the pistol.

"Dylan?"

There wasn't an answer.

He quickly finished and pulled up his pants.

Gabriel stood and simultaneously grabbed the handle of the bathroom door and took a deep breath. He pushed the handle down and then pushed the door open.

When he saw the boy being held in front of him with a gun to his head, he quickly raised his gun up and aimed it at the man.

Gabriel wasn't all the way out when the door came swinging toward him. It hit him in the face and sent him tumbling to the ground, and he nearly hit his head on the toilet when he fell back. His hand immediately went to his face and he felt his warm blood pooling at his nose, then confirmed he was bleeding when he looked down at his crimson hand.

When the door opened again, he looked up to see the barrel of his handgun pointed right between his eyes. He looked beyond the gun and his eyes went wide when he saw the man who was holding it. It was a familiar face, one that he could never forget. He'd seen the man's face many times over in his head the past couple of days, after he'd laid him out across the warehouse floor with the baseball bat.

"Oh, shit," Gabriel mumbled.

***

Will

After going out into the parking garage and helping Gabriel and Dylan safely depart, Will came back inside to meet with Holly and Marcus. Rachel, one of the survivors at the hospital who seemed to be running things from what Will could tell, had assigned each one of them their owns rooms. From what Will could see, there were plenty of open rooms, which made him and the others feel like they weren't intruding on the space of the hospital's existing group. Will put his few belongings in his room, and then went to Marcus' room where the three had agreed to meet.

When Will arrived, Holly was already inside the room waiting. She was sitting on the edge of the bed while Marcus was lying down, stretching his legs.

Will chuckled. "Something tells me that bed is probably more comfortable now than it would have been if you were here for other reasons."

Marcus smiled. "Yeah, you could say that."

Will took a seat in a chair with a thin and uncomfortable cushion.

"So," Will said.

"So, what are we going to do?" Holly asked, cutting straight to the chase.

Will and Marcus looked at each other, waiting for the other to speak. Will decided to go first.

"Do you think they're going to let us stay here?" Will

asked.

"I can't see them saying no, especially with your mom here," Holly said.

"They *could* kick us all out," Marcus said. "We don't know how much food and resources they have to go around."

Will shook his head. "No, I think Holly is right. Plus, my mom and that Jessica girl kept going on about what good people they are."

"I heard that Lawrence guy we met at that gas station is the one who's in charge here," Marcus said. "That's what that Brandon fella told me. Said he's out on a run picking up some supplies with one of the other survivors."

"Well, then, we should wait until he gets back, and we can meet with him and see where he's at on us staying here."

Marcus and Holly nodded. Holly then reached out to Will, and she was close enough for him to take her hand.

"How are you feeling?" she asked.

Will shrugged and put his head down, running his free hand through his hair. "*Relieved,* I guess, is the best word. I honestly wasn't sure if I was ever going to see either of my parents again. It's a little overwhelming."

A knock came at the door, and Jessica walked inside the room. Will saw her eyes go straight to his hand clasped with Holly's.

"Oh, sorry," Jessica said. It looked as if she was blushing.

"No, it's okay," Marcus said. "What's up?"

She looked over to Will. "I was hoping that I might be able to talk to you alone for a few minutes."

"Yeah, sure," Will said. He looked over to Holly. "Why don't you see if you can go get something to eat?"

"Okay, sweetie." Holly stood and then leaned down to give Will a kiss.

He smiled at her and watched as Marcus let her out of the room first, and then shut the door behind him as he exited.

***

Jessica

When Holly closed the door behind her, Jessica remained standing just a few feet inside the room. Will extended his hand, inviting her to sit down.

"I don't mind standing," Jessica said.

"Please, sit down. It'll make me more comfortable." Will was smiling as he said it. It was difficult for Jessica to look at him, as she could see Walt's resemblance so distinctly in him, especially in his eyes. Though she hadn't known the man but for a few hours, Walt was the only reason she was even standing in front of his son today. Walt would forever hold a place in her heart for what he'd done.

"Thanks for giving me a few minutes," Jessica said.

"It's not a problem. What's on your mind?"

Jessica drew in a deep breath. "Your mom, she's a sweet lady. We've both been through a lot over the last few days. Between what happened to your father, the accident, and her waking up from a coma... I'm just not really sure where she is mentally and emotionally."

"Yeah, I've been worried about that," Will said, looking down as he clasped his hands together. After a few moments, he looked back up to Jessica. "Thanks for taking care of her."

Jessica smiled. "She took care of me, too." Her smile then quickly turned into something somber as she began to cry. "I lost people I love this week, too, Will. Both of my parents."

"Oh, my God," Will said. "I'm so sorry."

Jessica nodded, wiping her eyes. "Your mother saved me from lying on the bed beside them and taking my own life. She fought with me, helped me move on."

Jessica felt Will's hand come over hers, and she grabbed onto his fingers as she continued to cry.

"I just want for her to be okay. She needs you."

"Sounds like she needs you just as much," Will added.

Jessica laughed and wiped her eyes again, also using her hand to move her hair from her face. She sniffled a few times, gathered herself, and then continued.

"There's something else I need to tell you about this place," Jessica said, wanting to tell him about the creature that was being held in the hospital.

Right as she was about to tell Will about what she'd seen, a scream came from the end of the hallway, closely followed by gunfire.

Jessica looked over to Will, who'd let go of her and jumped to his feet. He looked down to her.

"Get in the closet, now!" he demanded. "And stay there. Okay?"

Jessica nodded, breathing heavily now.

"Do it, now!" Will commanded her.

Jessica quickly got to her feet and got into the closet, shutting the door and trapping herself in total darkness.

CHAPTER TWENTY

David

David stood near the welcome counter. He held a shotgun in his hands while Cody and Trent stood behind him. Cody held a pistol to Gabriel's right temple, the hostage's hands bound with rope. Two of the nurses whose names David couldn't remember were in the receptionist area chatting, and screamed when the men came busting through the door. They continued to scream until David pumped the shotgun.

"Shut the fuck up!"

The two women trembled, but ceased their yelling.

"I've got a hostage!" David shouted, looking all around the hospital, calling everyone. "It's your friend, Gabriel! If you don't want us to blow his fucking head off, then I suggest you *all* come out right now!"

David moved to the doorway next to him, pointing the gun back toward the area where the kitchen was. In the short time he'd been at the hospital, there had always been people hanging out back there, and he was sure there would be now. He grinned when two very familiar faces appeared in front of him.

Marcus and Holly looked at David with their jaws wide open as he pointed the shotgun at them.

"David?" Marcus said. "How did you—"

"Shut the fuck up, Marcus! Just get your ass out here!"

David stood just outside of the doorway and their eyes didn't leave his as they passed by him and joined the rest of the group near the nurses' station.

More people followed behind them. Brandon, Kristen, Sarah, and Sam all followed.

"I've got a hostage. If any of you try anything, Cody back here won't even hesitate killing him."

"You alright, Gabriel?" Marcus asked.

David turned around and punched Gabriel's left cheek, and watched the man spit blood almost as soon as his fist had connected.

"David!" Marcus shouted. Next to him, Holly was in tears.

"You guys know each other?" Brandon asked.

Marcus looked at Brandon. "Yeah." Then he looked back toward David. "Yeah, we do."

"Where is everyone else?" David asked. "I know we're missing a few people. Surely, your friend Will is here, too." David looked back around the hospital. "Everyone else, come out!"

Almost simultaneously, Rachel came out of her room to his right and Trevor came out of an office to his left.

"Good," David said. "Gang's almost all here."

"What's going on here? Where's Lawrence?" Rachel asked.

"Lawrence that nigger we kilt?" Trent asked from behind David.

"Yeah." David said it without turning around to acknowledge Trent.

"Oh, my God," Rachel said. She covered her mouth and began to sob. David looked at the other survivors and could see the clear states of shock and disappointment in their faces.

"Where is he?" David asked.

"Where is who?" Holly asked.

He watched her tremble as he approached her, stopping just before he made contact with her. "You know *exactly* who. Where is Will?"

David looked up from Holly when he heard a voice coming from one of the rooms. He walked closer to the room he thought it was coming from and then the words became clearer.

"Will? Son, where are you?" There was a tremble in her voice.

David kicked down the door and saw the older woman lying on the bed.

"Son?" David asked, smiling.

The woman screamed.

***

Will

The scream of a woman echoed down the hall. Will had remained inside the room while he waited to try and get a grasp of what was happening outside, but knew he needed to go out and help.

"Stay put," Will told Jessica, who was still inside the closed closet. "Do not leave."

"Okay, I won't."

Will pushed the handle to the door down and stepped into the hallway.

He could see a group gathered at the end of the hallway,

near the entrance from the parking garage. Gabriel was surrounded by two men with guns. The other survivors of the hospital, including Holly and Marcus, stood near the welcome counter.

"Will!" The scream of his name came from his mother, and he ran to the room. Holly yelled something at him, but he ignored her.

When he looked inside the room, his mouth fell open.

"Surprised to see me, kid?" David Ellis asked.

The man had one arm wrapped around Will's mother, and he had a pistol to her head. Will looked over onto the bed and saw a shotgun lying there. Will eyed it.

"I dare you to try it," David said. "She'll be gone before you even get three steps over here."

Will looked back up to David. "She didn't do anything, David. It's me you want. Let her go."

David cocked his head. "And what makes you think that it's *you* that I want?"

"Just let her go, and we can go talk. It doesn't have to be like this."

David pushed Will's mother toward him, and he wrapped his arms around his sobbing and now only parent.

Will watched David push the pistol into its holster and then pick the shotgun up off of the bed, and then point it toward Will and his mother.

"I'll be the one telling y'all exactly how it's going to be. Now, move your asses out there with the others."

With his arm wrapped around his mother, Will made his way over to the others. Behind him, David kept pushing the barrel of the shotgun into his back.

"You can stop that. I get it," Will told David.

The pain shot right through Will's leg as the shotgun hit the back of his knee. He tumbled to the ground, taking his mother with him.

"Mom!"

Melissa lay on the ground, clutching her knee and writhing in pain. Will looked up to David.

"You son of a—"

The click of the shotgun being pumped resounded throughout the room, and Will stared down the barrel.

David stared right into Will's eyes and said, "Get... the fuck... up... now."

***

David

From what David could remember, the group standing in front of him represented all the survivors from the hospital, along with Will, Marcus, Holly, and Gabriel, who Cody was still holding at gunpoint.

David looked at Rachel. "Where do you keep all the weapons?"

Rachel looked confused. "What?"

"I know that you have a supply of weapons here and I know that you know where they are. Lawrence wouldn't let any outsiders in here with them, and no one ever carried them around the hospital. Where did he hide them?"

"I don't know," Rachel said, shuddering.

David let out a long sigh, withdrew the pistol from his waist, pointed it at Kristen's head, and pulled the trigger.

Everyone screamed as the young nurse fell limp and her body hit the floor, blood pooling from the wound just above her right eye.

"David!" Marcus yelled. He looked at David as if he could convince him to stop, but David knew he was no longer the same man that Marcus had once known.

Rachel was sobbing now as David looked back to her. "You still don't know where they are?"

"There's a service elevator in a restricted area," Rachel said, her words trembling. "One floor down, the elevator will take you out to a room that's secure. There's no creatures down there. There's a supply closet down there and that's where he keeps the guns. There isn't much, but what we have is down there."

"And what about yours?" David asked, looking at Marcus and Will.

"They're there, too," Brandon said. "We moved them in there just after these guys got here."

David looked over to Rachel. "Take me down there."

Rachel blushed. "I-I-I... I lost my access key. I was scared to tell Lawrence. Didn't think he would trust me anymore if he didn't think I was responsible enough to hold onto some keys."

As he reached into his pocket, David scoffed. He pulled out the keys he'd taken from Lawrence's corpse and waved them in front of his face. "Well, lucky for your friends here, I've got a set of keys. That may be the only thing that keeps me from shooting someone else."

***

Will

Will had helped his mother up off the floor and was now supporting her as she grimaced from the pain in her knee, though she assured him she'd be fine. One of the men behind David was wearing a backpack, and Will watched as he slipped the straps off of his shoulders and opened the main compartment. "Shit," Will mumbled.

The man was pulling out long, thick zip ties.

"What did you do with Dylan?" Holly asked.

"That pretty little boy? He gonna be *just* fine, don't y'all worry," the man with the backpack commented.

"You son of a bitch," Gabriel said. "If you—"

"Everyone, get down on your knees and put your hands behind your back!" David commanded the group, cutting Gabriel off. He looked over to Will's mother. "Let her stand. She'll be fine."

Will was reluctant, only glaring at David, who was looking back to him with a similar face. All Will wanted was to kill the David Ellis. He had regretted leaving David alive at the warehouse, but knew that Marcus and Holly would never have killed the man, considering all the history they had. Now, Will wondered if they were sharing the same regret.

"Just do it, Will," Marcus said.

"It's okay, son. My knee is feeling better. I can stand on my own," Melissa told him.

"Yeah... just do it, William." David was smiling now, and all it did was fuel the hate inside of Will.

In the end, Will did the thing that would at least temporarily keep him alive. He let go of his mother, turned around, and went to his knees like the others.

The man with David started at the far end of the line from Will, securing each prisoner's hands. Will could just barely hear the clicks the plastic zip ties made over the crying of the four women in the group.

"On your feet," David demanded. Will was standing before the others in his group were.

He watched David look back to the man who had been holding Gabriel hostage before they'd had him join the others.

"Take this guy and go down to the storage closet," David said to one of the other men in his group, nodding toward Trevor. He then looked over to Brandon. "Do you have the keys to the ambulance?"

Brandon nodded. "They're still in my pocket."

David looked over to the other man in his group and nodded. The man walked over to Brandon and removed the keys from his pocket while David kept the shotgun aimed directly at Brandon's head. He then looked back over to the man was holding Gabriel.

"Alright, Cody, go down there with her and start taking the guns to the ambulance."

David then looked Will right in the eyes. "I have something special to show these folks."

CHAPTER TWENTY-ONE

Will

David and one of the men he came with, whose name Will now knew to be Trent, led the group down the hallway of the hospital. They passed room after room that the survivors had been staying in until they reached the end of the hall. Will looked one direction and saw a set of four elevators. Each one of them had signs posted on the doors that warned against using them. When he looked the other way, he saw a set of double doors with small windows on them that Will was unable to see through because of the darkness on the other side.

"Through the doors," David directed them from the back of the group.

Will was near the middle of the pack with Holly to his right and Marcus directly in front of him. The group followed his instructions, and Rachel was the first to push through the double doors, as everyone else followed.

"I think you know exactly where we're going, don't you?" David shouted to Rachel at the front of the group. "Go on, take us there."

"Where is he taking us?" Will asked Rachel.

"Tell him and I'll start shooting," David said. "I want it to be a surprise."

Will took a deep breath, trying to contain his frustration.

He wiggled his hands in the restraints with little hope of getting out. David had made sure that his zip tie was extra tight, so much so that it was now cutting off the circulation and he was losing feeling in his wrists.

The group entered a dark corridor and Will could feel his heart thump in his chest. He wondered where David could be taking the group to where it needed to be a surprise. Just behind him, he could hear his mother sobbing. Will slowed down enough for her to catch up to where he was walking.

"It's okay, Mom."

"I'm scared, Will," Melissa said, her eyes red from crying.

"I know. So am I. But you're going to be fine." In truth, Will really wasn't sure if they were going to make it through this. He knew what a monster that David Ellis was, and he knew that the man would get off from toying with them. How much longer until he would finally get bored and decide to do away with them?

"I'm not scared for me. I'm scared for you, son."

"Don't be. It's going to be fine, Mom."

"She should be scared for you," David said from behind them. He jammed the barrel of the shotgun into the small of Will's back, causing him to grimace. Will heard him chuckle before he did it again. Fed up with it, Will finally turned around and stood inches from David's face.

"Do it, then! Just go ahead and shoot!"

"Will!" Holly yelled. Like his mother, she was crying and had a shudder in her voice.

"Do it!" Will shouted again.

Before Will could react, David threw a punch catching Will under his left eye. He hit a wall before falling to the ground, unable to brace himself with his hands bound behind his back. He felt the blood pool in his mouth and used his tongue to check for any teeth missing. Still, he was only missing the tooth he'd lost as a teenager playing hockey.

"That'd be too fucking easy," David said. "Now, get on your God damned feet."

Spitting blood onto the white tile floor, Will slowly made his way back to his knees. Before he could get to his feet, David kicked him in his ribs, sending him back down to the ground.

Will coughed, trying to catch his breath as more blood came from his mouth. He made it to his knees again, and this time, David let him stand all the way.

"Now, fucking move," David said, pressing the shotgun back into Will's spine.

They reached the end of another hallway and only had the option to go left. This area of the hospital looked much like the one the group was living in, rooms on either side, most of them closed.

When Will moved around the corner, he saw a light shining at the end of the hallway. The entire group was being quiet, aside from the sobs of his mother and Holly. As they reached the end of the hall, Will heard a sound that was all too familiar. His eyes widened. His heartbeat sped up.

When they went around another corner at the end of the hall, Will saw the source of the light.

Inside a small room with a large window at the front, there was an Empty, strapped to a bed, fighting to get out of its restraints.

"What is this doing here?" Will asked.

David pointed down to the other end of the group. "Ask her."

Will looked and saw the rest of the group already looking at Rachel.

She licked her lips. "We... we've been studying her. Running tests and such. Trying to see what we can find out about them."

"What have you found out?" Holly asked.

"Only that the disease isn't viral. We ran many tests and couldn't find any signs that she's ill. Other than that, nothing much."

"What do you think is making them like that?" Will asked.

"We don't know," Brandon added. "We were supposed to run some more tests with Lawrence tonight." He looked over to David. "Guess that won't be happening now."

"Guess not," David said, laughing right after the words came out.

Will watched as David walked past him. He walked to the end of the line and stopped in front of Rachel. At first, she gasped when he unsheathed his knife. Then, David cut through her zip tie, and Rachel rubbed her burning wrists.

"Remove the restraints," David told her.

"What?" Rachel asked, as if she hadn't heard the question.

"The creature in there, let it go."

"Um, okay. Let me just go and get a sedat—"

"No," David said.

Her jaw dropped and tears welled up her eyes again. "Please."

"Don't do this, David," Marcus said.

David moved within inches of Marcus' face. Will thought about making a move, almost forgetting that there was another man in the room with a gun pointed at them.

"Or what, Marcus? You gonna pretend like everything is okay and then just leave me for dead again?"

"Mother fucker, you shot me!"

"Yeah, and you fucking deserved it. I saved your God damned life and you fucking betrayed me. I should have just left you in that room to rot."

Will almost spoke up after hearing David trying to take the credit for saving Marcus, but decided against it.

"Now," David said, turning his attention back to Rachel. "Go in there and undo her restraints."

Will looked on as Rachel began to tremble. The tears were pouring out of her eyes now, and she was trying to say something that couldn't be made out through how upset she was.

The nurse standing next to Rachel was crying as well, and Will watched as David put the shotgun into her chest.

"You can either do as I say, and go in there and let that thing go, or you can watch as I put a slug in this bitch's chest. Then, we can all wait around and see what happens after she's dead for a while."

David pumped the shotgun, and Sarah screamed. Inside the small room, the creature was snarling and writhing in the bed, trying desperately to get out of the restraints.

"Okay, okay," Rachel finally said. She made her way to the door and started to type the code to enter it, but her hand was moving around too much from her nerves to allow her to hit the buttons. As David counted down from five, giving her a time limit before he'd presumably fire, Rachel finally punched in the code and the door clicked and the light turned from red to green.

She hesitated before she walked through the door, the snarl of the creature louder now that she had pushed the door to where it was cracked. Will could see from her profile that her eyes were closed and her mouth was moving, and he assumed that she was praying.

Finally, Rachel pushed the door all the way open and walked through. The growl of the creature became more rampant, and it chomped its jaws as Rachel approached the bed. When she'd made it about halfway to the bed, Rachel turned around and looked at David.

"Please, don't make me do this."

"Alright," David said. He pressed the shotgun against Sarah's chest again, who screamed and continued to cry.

"Don't!" Rachel yelled.

Marcus looked over to David. "Stop it!"

Trent was laughing as David looked back at Rachel and started counting. "Three, two..."

"Okay, okay! Stop!" Rachel said.

She turned around again and walked up to the Empty's left leg. It spit and snarled at her as she unbound the leather strap that was around its ankle. When it was all the way undone, the beast kicked its leg, which startled Rachel and made her jump back, almost sending her down onto the ground. Will looked over when he heard Trent begin to laugh again.

Rachel crept back up to the body and made her way to the

Empty's right arm. Will assumed she was going to use a criss-cross pattern to unbind the creature so that it would stay somewhat contained. If she went ahead and unstrapped the right leg, the thing would be able to maneuver much easier.

Just as she got the strap undone, she tried to move back as quickly as she could, but she wasn't fast enough. The creature grabbed her, and Rachel screamed. Its jaws chomped more rapidly, but it was unable to keep a grasp on her and she backed up until she hit a small table behind her. Will watched as she looked back at the table and saw the array of surgical tools that were lying on it. She stared at the scalpels and other tools for a few moments before David spoke.

"Don't even think about it. If you stab that thing, everyone out here is dead, and so are you."

Rachel gripped the side of the table and closed her eyes, trying to fight off more oncoming tears from what Will could tell. She took another deep breath and then moved back down to the foot of the bed to undo the other leg.

The Empty reached for her and Will couldn't even begin to imagine how terrified she was. Though he didn't know the woman, he did have an understanding of how sick and twisted David Ellis was, and he felt for Rachel, knowing that anything could happen next.

Almost as soon as the creature's leg was released, it kicked and reached for Rachel. The thing looked almost as if it was having a seizure, wanting nothing except to get to Rachel. Because that is all the Empties wanted: to feed on human flesh.

"She's never going to get that arm undone," Will mumbled to himself. Holly apparently heard him, looking over to him with her eyes full of tears.

Rachel made her way to the bound left hand, but stopped when the creature rolled over and tried to grab her. When it did, it rolled all the way off of the bed. The creature's arm bent a strange way, and Will heard the snap and saw the hand rip away as the thing disappeared onto the floor.

Rachel screamed and ran for the door.

Just as she came through the doorway, David grabbed onto her and threw her back into the room. He pulled the pistol from his holster and fired a shot into her leg. Will couldn't see where the bullet hit her, but she screamed out and fell to the ground. He watched as David pulled the door shut.

"David!" Holly screamed, crying.

"This isn't who you are, David," Marcus said. "I know you. Please, let her out. Open the door."

David reared back and punched Marcus square in the nose, sending him down to the ground. Without his hands to catch him, Marcus hit his head against the tile floor and then didn't move.

"You don't know shit," David mumbled.

Everyone in the group was crying now except for Will and the apparently unconscious Marcus.

Will looked back into the room when he heard the loud snarl. The Empty was on its feet and free from the restraints. Its arm was bent the wrong way and had torn near the wrist, freeing the beast.

All the others screamed.

And as the beast fell down to the ground, Will turned his head, listening to the creature tear into Rachel as her screams slowly trailed off into silence.

CHAPTER TWENTY-TWO

David

He laughed. For five minutes straight, his eyes never moved from the scene unfolding before his eyes. The thing that finally brought him away from watching the human flesh torn apart in front of him was the radio on his belt.

"We've got it all loaded," Cody said through the radio.

"Excellent," David said.

"It wasn't a lot of stuff, but it'll be a good add-on to what we already got. You guys ready?"

"Meet Trent and me in the main hallway. And do what you've got to do." David smiled after saying the last line, hoping that Cody would take the hint and shoot Trevor, the man he'd chosen to send with Cody to gather the guns.

David turned around and looked at the group. He enjoyed seeing the look of shock on their faces. The only regret he had was that Marcus, the traitor, was knocked out and couldn't see what he'd done.

"We've gotta get going," Trent said.

Across the hall, a door was cracked open. David walked over to the room, keeping the shotgun aimed at the group. He looked toward Brandon, who was at the end of the line closest to him, and signaled him inside the room.

"Come on, in you go."

Brandon slowly walked over to the room and went inside.

David had already signaled to Sarah, who Brandon had been standing beside.

"Come on, everyone, fall in line," David ordered.

The others made their way toward the room, and David looked over to Trent.

"He can stay," David said, nodding his head toward Will.

Trent grabbed Will by his arms and kept him in the center of the hallway.

Holly and Will's mother stopped, and turned back to Will.

"No!" Holly cried.

"Go, it's fine," Will told her.

She ran over to Will and put her head onto his chest. He nestled his head with hers awkwardly, and David could see Holly trying desperately to free her hands so that she could embrace Will. She looked up and kissed Will on his lips.

"Alright, break it up. Come on, Holly," David said.

She pulled away from Will's lips and turned to David, her cheeks flush and her eyes crimson. She walked toward him, looking back at Will.

"I love you," she said.

"I love you, too."

Holly then looked up at David.

"Aww," he said.

Holly stopped right in front of him. "If you hurt him, we *will* find you, and we *will* kill you."

David laughed, grabbed her arm, and threw her into the room. She fell on the ground face first.

"You son of a bitch!" Will yelled.

David Ellis only continued to laugh.

Now, it was just Will and his mother in the hallway. She

wasn't moving, only standing in the center of the hallway with Will, staring at him.

"I can't leave you, son. I can't do this again."

"It's okay, Mom. Just go."

"No," David said. They looked over to him just as he turned around and shut the door, Holly's sobbing still resonating from inside the room. "She can stay."

There was no emotion on Will's face, but from where David stood, he could see him swallow hard. He made his way over to Will, who wasn't putting up any kind of a fight with Trent. To an extent, David did admire Will. The look on his face was that of a man who wasn't scared and who had accepted his fate.

David smiled as he moved within inches of Will's face. "I'm sorry, but this is going to be extremely painful. A pain like you've never experienced or could ever imagine."

Will scoffed. "You're not sorry."

David chuckled. "No, I'm really not."

As soon as the words came out, David took the butt of the shotgun and jammed it into Will's stomach.

Will bent over and coughed, unable to clutch his stomach. He gasped for air.

"Will!" his mother yelled. She tried to go to him, but David held her back. "Let me go!"

But, the old woman was no match for his strength.

"Bring him," David told Trent, and he walked Will's mother over toward the room where the Empty was still feasting on the flesh of Rachel. The sound of it was music to David Ellis' ears, but Will's mother turned away and was writhing in his arms, trying to escape. Preoccupied with its meal, the creature never looked back at them.

David let the woman go, and she ran to her son, burying her head into his chest just like Holly had done. Now, Will was crying, and it brought a new sensation into David's blood to see the man distraught.

With his mother soaking his shirt, Will looked at David, gritting his teeth, and said, "You do what you've gotta do."

David nodded and opened the door. The snarl of the beast got louder, but it surprisingly didn't look back at them. He left the door open and walked over to Will.

When he reached Will, he smiled at him again. "You really shouldn't have left me for dead. We could still be back at my building, thriving. But no, you had to go and fuck everything up. Now, I'm going to make you feel every bit of pain I felt."

"Fuck you," Will said, his eyes beginning to redden from the tears.

David scoffed. "No, fuck you, kid."

Will gasped as his mom continued to cry and yell into his chest, and he waited for David to grab him and throw him into the room.

"Hold him tight," David said, looking to Trent.

Will cocked his head.

David grabbed onto Will's mother's arm, and pulled her away from her son. She started to fight him and scream louder, so he dropped the shotgun and picked her up around the waist with both his hands.

"No!" Will screamed.

David was in front of the open door now, and he saw the Empty inside the room finally look up from Rachel's mangled and unrecognizable body.

Will was bucking Trent, who kept a tight hold on him.

David looked over to Will and said, “Yes.”

He threw Will’s mother into the room and shut the door.

Then, he hurried over to Will and moved Trent out of the way, taking Will and throwing him against the window.

“Watch!” David told him.

The window was fogging up from where Will was breathing heavily into it, and his eyes were wetting the glass as they were pressed up against it.

Inside the room, his mother didn’t stand a chance.

The Empty was on its feet, and it only took moments for it to pounce on the old woman. She screamed as she fell to the ground, the creature over her and sinking its decrepit teeth into her left shoulder.

Will became limp in David’s arms, as if every ounce of hope had left his body. All David could do was smile, and he felt a tingle inside from watching the young man in so much agony.

“You son of a bitch!” Will cried with his face pressed against the glass. “You son of a bitch, I’m gonna kill you!”

Without responding, David pulled back Will’s head by his hair, and slammed his face against the glass. He let Will go, letting his listless body hit the floor, leaving a bloodstain on the window.

And when he looked to the blood dripping down the glass, he saw Will’s mother’s hand stop moving, as the creature ripped out her throat, looking into the air and growling as it chewed.

***

Jessica

The tiny closet had just enough space for Jessica to sit down and tuck her knees to her chest. The silence had become nearly deafening as she was surrounded by the darkness. All she'd thought about since Will had left the room was her own exit, but she decided to listen to what he'd demanded of her and stay inside the closet.

After an extended drought of any sound, she finally heard something. Jessica held in her breath so as not to try and make an ounce of noise. The footsteps stopped in front of her room, and she heard a man clear his throat.

About thirty seconds had passed when more footsteps echoed from further down the hall. Jessica shuddered as her heart thumped inside her chest.

"Glad you all could make it," the voice right outside of her room said.

The other footsteps were almost to her room now, and she could tell from the rhythm that it was more than one person. They came to a stop in front of her room.

"You got everything loaded up?" The voice sounded slightly familiar to Jessica, but she couldn't quite picture the face.

"Yeah, we're good to go."

"Where's the guy that helped you?" This was a different voice than the other two, but sounded uneducated, like the man who'd originally been standing at the door.

Jessica heard one of the men rustling with something on his body, then one of the more ignorant men said, "Woooo, God damn. You gut 'em?"

"Slit his fuckin' throat, I did."

The man with the more articulate voice spoke next. “Now that I’ve, hopefully, gained your trust and shown you where my allegiance lies, where is your camp that we’re going to?”

There was a moment of silence before one of the men answered. “It’s at an old farm and slaughterhouse. Hopkins Farm. Just outside of the city.”

“They take that boy there?” the well-spoken man asked.

“Yeah, I reckon they did.”

“These people gonna be lookin’ for him,” the other hillbilly said.

“They’ll never find him.”

The two men shared a laugh until Jessica heard two gunshots, followed by consecutive thumps. She had to cover her mouth to keep herself from screaming.

“Idiots,” the man with the articulate voice said. And when he spoke this time, the face finally creeped into her head. Something about how soft he had said the word jarred her memory. She remembered walking down the hall and seeing the man with the cold eyes sitting on the bed. Then later, he’d spoken to her in the kitchen and she’d read him to be someone dangerous. She saw his dark curly blonde hair, and his bright eyes that somehow reflected his darkness.

“Hello? Hello? Are you there? Over.” There was a tremble in the man’s voice that hadn’t been there before. He sounded scared.

“Trent? Cody?” This voice came through what sounded like a two-way radio.

“This is David.”

“What’s your position, David?”

“I’m just now getting out of the hospital. I’ve got some of

the weapons with me. But, Trent and Cody... they didn't make it. The bastards here shot them."

There was silence. Jessica's mouth was wide open and she could hear David chuckle to himself as he waited for a response from the person on the other end.

"Get your ass back here and we'll figure out what we're going to do. Head on I-40 West and take the Waverly Road exit. That's the exit where that gas station was we found you at earlier. Head another two miles down that road and you'll see us waiting on you."

"Al-alright, I'll get there as soon as I can."

And as she heard his footsteps begin to fade away and a door open in the distance, the face of a man who'd been saved and brought here, just like her, was now etched into her mind as a killer. She finally stood, opened the closet, and walked through the door, out into the hallway.

***

Jessica knew there was only one place the group could be. She ran down the main hallway, through the double doors, and then down the dark hallway that led back to where the creature was.

As she approached, she slowed to a walk when she heard people shouting, and she picked up her pace again.

When she came around the corner, she stopped. On the floor, Will was curled up, crying with his cheek pressed against the tile. She could also see Marcus, who was sitting up against a wall, not moving. She focused her attention back to Will and ran to his side.

"Oh, my God. What happened?"

Will didn't answer. He only continued to sob onto the

floor. She noticed his hands were bound and Jessica tried to console him by putting her hand on him, but he didn't react. It was as if he didn't even know she was there. Behind her, she could hear what sounded like the rest of the group calling for help inside of a small room.

When she stood up to go help them, she was facing the lit room where the creature had been. Before turning around, her eyes naturally looked into the room, and Jessica saw her.

Melissa.

The creature was hollowing out Melissa Kessler's stomach, while the woman lay motionless with her wide-open eyes looking to the ceiling. Her throat had been ripped open, but her face was still intact. The tears came pouring from Jessica's eyes, and she immediately crumbled to the ground next to Will.

She lay next to him on her stomach, not even concerned with her injured shoulder. Even with the people yelling out from inside the room behind her, Jessica couldn't block out the sound of the monster inside the room feasting on her friend. But, next to her, Will Kessler's words were becoming clear.

"I'll fucking kill him. I'll fucking kill him. I'll fucking kill him!"

EPILOGUE

Dylan

When the trunk opened, there were three men and a woman waiting to pull him out. He recognized only one of the men from the gas station they'd abducted him from. He'd screamed so loud all the way here that he was too hoarse to even cry out, and his hand hurt from repeatedly pounding the inside of the trunk.

"Come'on you little shit," one of the men said as he reached down toward Dylan.

"No, wait," the woman said, grabbing onto the man's arm.

She reached into her back pocket and pulled out a bandana. She folded it to where it was long and rectangular.

"Hold him," she said.

Two of the men reached down and pinned Dylan as he tried to break free, yelling out. His hands were restrained, but he still had a lot of fight in him, especially for a child. The woman managed to get the bandana around his eyes as a makeshift blindfold, and then the men lifted him up and out of the trunk of the car.

"Where are you taking me?" Dylan asked as they dragged him through grass.

None of the people responded.

"Please, where are—"

He felt a hand hit him in the back of the head.

"Shut the fuck up!" one of the men demanded.

Dylan cried harder now, and he fell down onto the ground.

"Get his ass up," the woman said.

He felt hands under his arms and he was on his feet again. Then one of the people grabbed his shoulders and he could feel their warm, stank breath hit his face.

One of the men spoke. "You pull that shit again, I'll start cuttin' them little God damn fingers off, you understand me, boy?"

As he trembled, Dylan nodded.

They continued to walk until they finally stopped, and Dylan heard the protracted squeak of what sounded like a large door opening.

"Come on," one of the male voices instructed.

They started walking again, presumably entering the door that had just opened. Dylan listened carefully and heard the muffled cries of others.

"Well, hello again," one of the male voices said. When he did, the indistinct cries became louder.

"Hello?" Dylan called out.

"Gag this little prick," one of the men said.

"No, please don't," Dylan cried, but before he knew it, one of the people was stuffing a sock into his mouth.

He tried to speak, but it only came out as garbled and inarticulate.

As he felt a chill in his arms, and his chest hurt from the stress his little heart was putting on him, he heard the rattling of metal in front of him.

"Bring him here," a male voice said.

A push on his back forced him over toward the voice, and then he felt one of the people force his arms straight up.

Some kind of shackles were clamped around one of his wrists, and he gripped onto the chain that they were attached to. He used his free arm to fight and tried yelling out, until a backhand slap across his face stopped him, and he let his head fall to his chest as they restrained his other arm, leaving him hanging in the middle of the place with his feet barely touching the ground.

Dylan felt the blood around his lips. Laughing and talking amongst themselves, the people walked away from him, back toward the way they'd come in.

He heard the door shut and their voices fade, leaving him hanging there while the people next to him tried to scream through their gags.

Dylan looked up for a moment, before letting his head fall again and passing out.

TO BE CONTINUED...

Want to be the first to know when the next book is coming out?

Join my new release mailing list for news, exclusive content, members only giveaways and contests, and more! You'll get a free gift just for signing up.

VISIT:

www.zachbohannon.com

THE WITNESS

A Slasher Horror Novel

For fans of *Friday the 13th*, *The Texas Chainsaw Massacre*, *House of 1,000 Corpses*, and *Halloween*

Visit:

http://bit.ly/witnessbook

ACKNOWLEDGEMENTS

Thank you to all the readers who came across Empty Bodies on Amazon and took a chance on it.

Thank you, Taylor Krauss and Meghan Cowhan.

Thanks, Johnny for another amazing cover.

Thanks to my friends in the author community:
J. Thorn, David J. Delaney, Dan Padavona, Richard Brown, Mat Morris, Michelle Read, Wade Finnegan, Xavier Granville, C.C. Wall, John Oakes, Simon Whistler, Robert Chazz Chute, Carl Sinclair, Darren Wearmouth, T.W. Piperbrook, J. Scott Sharp, and Nancy Elliot Pertu

WHAT DID YOU THINK OF *ADAPTATION?*

For independent authors like myself, reviews are very important. You won't see my books at the grocery store or on some famous television personality's book list. Reviews help new readers discover our work so that they can enjoy our stories and we can write more books.

If you enjoyed this book, I would be forever grateful if you would take the time to click the link below and just leave a few words about what you thought about Empty Bodies 2 on Amazon. This link will take you right there:

http://bit.ly/eb2reviews

And if you have any questions or comments regarding this title, or anything else for that matter, I'd love to hear from you. Please feel free to e-mail me at info@zachbohannon.com. I personally respond to every e-mail.

ABOUT THE AUTHOR

Something about the dark side of life has always appealed to me. Whether I experience it through reading and watching horror or listening to my favorite heavy metal bands, I have been forever fascinated with the shadow of human emotion.

While in my 20's, I discovered my passion to create through playing drums in two heavy metal bands: Kerygma and Twelve Winters. While playing in Twelve Winters (a power metal band with a thrash edge fronted by my now wife Kathryn), I was able to indulge myself in my love of writing by penning the lyrics for all our music. My love of telling a story started here, as many of the songs became connected to the same concept and characters in one way or another.

Now in my 30's, my creative passion is being passed to

willing readers through the art of stories. While I have a particular fascination for real life scenarios, I also love dark fantasy. So, you'll find a little bit of everything in my stories, from zombies to serial killers, angels and demons to mindless psychopaths, and even ghosts and parallel dimensions.

My influences as a writer come primarily from the works of Clive Barker, Stephen King, and Blake Crouch in the written form; the beautifully dark, rich lyrics of Mikael Akerfeldt from the band Opeth; and an array of movies, going back to the root of my fascination at a young age with 70's and 80's slasher films such as *Halloween, Friday the 13th,* and *The Texas Chainsaw Massacre.*

I live in Nashville, Tennessee with my wife Kathryn, our daughter Haley, and our German Shepherd Guinness. When I'm not writing, I enjoy playing hockey, watching hockey and football, cycling, watching some of my favorite television shows and movies, and, of course, reading.

Connect with me online:

Website: www.zachbohannon.com
Subscribe: http://bit.ly/zbbjoin
Facebook: http://www.facebook.com/zbbwrites
Pinterest: http://www.pinterest.com/zbbwrites
Twitter: @zachbohannon32
Instagram: @zachbohannon

KEEP ON READING!

For a complete list of Zach Bohannon's books on Amazon, please visit:

http://bit.ly/zachbohannonbooks

Printed in Great Britain
by Amazon